OKPsyche

a novel

Anya Johanna DeNiro

Small Beer Press
Easthampton, MA

Small Beer Press
150 Pleasant Street #306
Easthampton, MA 01027
smallbeerpress.com
weightlessbooks.com
bookmoonbooks.com
info@smallbeerpress.com

Distributed to the trade by Consortium.

Library of Congress Cataloging-in-Publication Data

Names: DeNiro, Anya Johanna, 1973- author.
Title: OKPsyche : a novel / Anya Johanna DeNiro.
Description: First edition. | Easthampton, MA : Small Beer Press, [2023] |
    Summary: "An unnamed trans woman is looking for a sense of belonging, a
    better relationship with her son, and friends that aren't imaginary in
    this playful and aching short novel"-- Provided by publisher.
Identifiers: LCCN 2023006848 (print) | LCCN 2023006849 (ebook) | ISBN
    9781618732088 (paperback) | ISBN 9781618732095 (ebook)
Subjects: LCGFT: Transgender fiction. | Novels.
Classification: LCC PS3604.E58446 O47 2023 (print) | LCC PS3604.E58446
    (ebook) | DDC 813/.6--dc23/eng/20230421
LC record available at https://lccn.loc.gov/2023006848
LC ebook record available at https://lccn.loc.gov/2023006849

First edition 1 2 3 4 5 6 7 8 9

Set in Georgia and FrugalSans.
Printed on 50# Natures Natural 30% PCR recycled paper by the Versa Press, East Peoria, IL.
"Psyche Asleep in a Landscape," Karl Joseph Aloys Agricola, 1837, metmuseum.org.

For trans folks, again and again.

"And it's inside myself that I must create someone who will understand."

—Clarice Lispector

I.

You have struggled for a long time as to whether you have a soul or not—whether anyone does—or if you're only a gathering of restless and ginned-up personality traits brought together to fool yourself into believing that there is, in fact, a you. As opposed to an unrecognizable someone-else.

This is complicated by the fact that you used to be someone else entirely.

On days when your life has a sense of purpose and direction—and also, especially, when no one stares at you too long or whispers or laughs at you on the street or in Home Depot when you're buying gallons of paint called Autumn Dream and Etruscan Sugar—the soul makes itself felt, and that essence you think you have takes hold of you. You become willingly possessed by yourself. And you allow yourself to take flight.

However, on days when nothing goes right and you seem to be walking into an abyss no matter which direction you take—and in the suburbs, all directions are more or less the same—you become convinced that there can be no such thing as the soul. On those days, you crumble under gazes and snickers.

The answer has to rest in something that's not a mere mood—and moreover, not dependent on the cruel whims of passersby, whose own ensoulment is conditional on whether they treat you like a human being. You have vowed to move past that, particularly when you go through the cadences of the everyday as a woman living alone with a cat, estranged from nearly every aspect of the life you used to have.

You can't deny it hurts when, after paying for and loading up the groceries in your cart at the Hy-Vee, the older woman behind you in line snickers with the cashier, and tries to draw the cashier into an exercise in quick bonding. *Can you believe these men, dressing up? Can you? What will men think of next?*

You leave, head down, before you can find out if the cashier relents.

But perhaps both conditions—soul, no soul—are right, in their own time and fashion. You can't imagine it being somewhere *in the middle.* A blurry middle does nothing for you. You've worked way too hard to escape that middle. You live in fear that you'll be yanked back there by others. *Pull yourself together, why don't you.*

Perhaps the soul disappears and reappears like a light being turned on and off as conditions warranted. So it goes.

Look at yourself. You can't make that shit up.

Errands: a project that just might save you after all. You need more primer and you need to return Autumn Dream to the Home Depot. Your human hair wig unfurls in the bathroom sink like a sea anemone. Predatory strawberry blonde. The beech trees in the front yard are still dormant, the sap thick and cold. The snow on the ground, in many places, has taken on a dirty, ruddy sheen, like the coat of a cocker spaniel who needs a bath. You gently roll your wig up in a towel. You are repainting your son's old room. Covering over the stick figures in green marker and the tape remnants from Transformers posters that hadn't hung there in two years, to make the walls bare again on the off-chance that one day the eleven-year-old will stay overnight with you for a simple sleepover. After you were let go at the health care company—termination for unspecified reasons—you decided to freelance from home, become a consultant. Already the savings are almost gone. You empty the old coffee into the dirty sink like expunging the black blood of a minotaur. Your son lives one state away.

When you leave your house it starts snowing big snow-globe flakes. You didn't realize it was going to snow and you are unprepared in your garb. Ballet flats are a bad choice until April or May. The retiree neighbors glare at you in their driveways as you exit the house—your half-real state of suspicion boomerangs back to you. The gales fan the snow onto the sidewalks, the trees, the cars, the parking garages. Under the eaves of the condominiums, sparrows dart out and fly back under shelter again, as if they can't believe what's happening. It is late March. For you, the seasons wobble. The razor nicks on your legs leave marks like red stars. They never fade. Here is the constellation the Irate Swan; here is the Father Who Says He's Embarrassed by You. Hard to navigate by. These are obscured by black leggings and a long skirt. You also wear a jean jacket, and a layer of foundation, but not too much around the eyes. You don't want any trouble—looking too "pretty" at a hardware store would be a dead giveaway. You can't afford surgery to soften your features, to break and drain the jaw like a polder, to tuck the cheeks. A face remade to offer comfort to normal strangers in the afternoons all passing by you in farmers' markets, state parks, the Gap. You had acquaintances in your old support group who'd cry when they look at themselves in the mirror, at the lack they thought was self-evident there.

You understand this and you have done it count-less times yourself, using a microscope that no one else possessed upon your hairline and your hips.

As part of your self-care regimen, you resist avoiding mirrors.

At you wait a minute at the Home Depot paint counter, you watch the big snow-globe flakes melt on your coat. The sales associate has the same name as your father.

"I need to return this paint." You stare at the sales associate's face. Heave the can onto the counter. His apron's splattered with so much paint that it looks like a rainbow bled out in his arms from a gunshot wound. You imagine him catching walleye like your father, edge of the dock, holding up the flailing fish still on the hook—

"Which paint."

"Autumn Dream. It's the color . . . not the right hue for the wall, even with the primer—"

"No returns." The associate with your father's name doesn't meet you in the eye, and his gaze skitters around.

4

Okay, you know where this is going, where it has already gone. "No, look, I've read the return policy."

"Do you really think people aren't going to laugh at you?"

"Excuse me?"

"Behind your back. They might pretend . . . but they're just humoring you, at best. Also what kind of role model are you for your son?"

I almost never see my son, you want to say. *He's in Kansas with my ex.*

Instead, you start shaking. "I'd like to speak to the manager, please."

"Don't try to change the subject. Don't cut me off. Show some respect."

You close your eyes. Usually, it's better to simply defer to the strong course of the inerrancy of strangers. You need to walk. You leave the paint can and wander over to the lumber section on the other side of the store, past the popcorn machine, past the sliding doors leading outside to the gardening section where all the products of spring—azaleas, soil, seed package displays—have a light crust of wet snow upon them, past the power tools whirling, past the checkout lanes and the cashiers who may or may not be staring at you.

You don't care. You stop in front of planks.

The paint associate has followed a couple of steps behind you, and when you stop, he stops about a foot from you.

"Don't you walk away from me like that. I haven't finished saying what I wanted to say. Have you ever thought about what your mother thinks about you? And what her neighbors think of her, because of you?"

At last you simply cannot take another word. "Shut up and help me load this wood into the car."

He pauses. "What do you have, a fucking Prius? It's not going to fit."

"Your truck then. You have a truck, right?"

Several minutes pass in which all of the pagings of sales associates swirl around you.

"Yeah."

The truck has a "Ron Paul 2012" bumper sticker, and a terrible paint job on the hood, where green house paint covers over rust spots like Astroturf over a minefield. The sparrows under the eaves of the parking garage are gone. You drive the truck. You'll take an Uber to get your Prius later, you reason. The sales associate sleeps in the passenger seat, cheek plastered on the frosty glass like Silly Putty.

Learn about this one weird unbelievable trick for finding your family.

You used to do UX writing for biotech websites, which was sort of like discovering a sinkhole inside a sinkhole. When you were in the midst of your great and awesome change, there were men you worked with who were inexorably good. You were terrified of them. Men your age in cubicles next to you. They were patient and a bit pedantic. They were good guys. And the fact that they had ordinary pains, doubts, regrets, and the like only made you more resentful of them. You did not want to be seen as one of them, purely an ordinary man, a good family man, a good father (even though you were a reasonably good father), prudent with money, never expressing too strong an opinion, always willing to be helpful, slightly awkward, forthright in all matters, a bit long-winded, and unmemorable in nearly everything. But more than that, being *satisfied* with unmemorability, to court it and have no regrets, except for the minor regrets that inevitably cropped up when the mind drifted—for example, when stuck in traffic—such as that vacation to Disneyland he should have taken with the family instead of staying home during that two-week stretch in the summer of 2__, when he wasn't sure about the recession and its effects on his employment; he was being cautious but the kids would have loved it. They did not drink in excess, they rarely raised a cross word, they were not emotionally manipulating their spouses. They were not causing trouble. They did not cause fights. They worked hard but were not wholly driven by their jobs. Their passions were for cars (although not expensive sports cars), board games, gadgets. In their lives they were afforded the opportunity to pursue these passions. They knew they were generally liked, and could hold this as a certainty, a baseline with which to pursue their interests. The thought of being considered one of these men—even though you had disguised yourself to look exactly like one of them—made you viscerally sick.

You've wondered sometimes: is their goodness a form of evil? No, no, it can't be—there is something obscene about you even thinking it. But it had made you upset that you were prohibited by societal norms not to feel livid at them, when you were in the midst of becoming yourself. Three years ago in the men's room mirror in that office complex, you stared at your stubbled face with fear, and confusion, with the soft rock ambience around you, and when you were sure nobody would be coming through the door, you adjusted the edge of your lace panties. You'd order them in bulk online and have them sent to your job.

While the sales associate unloads the wood from his truck and brings it into your son's bedroom, you go inside your kitchen, put a mug of hot water in the microwave for English breakfast tea. You are ready for what's about to happen: you had a dream about it last week. And you know what you have to build with that lumber, with the plans that you had received in the mail the day after your dream, from a slender air mail envelope with no postage. The return address only said ORIOLE, and the address was smudged.

After the lumber is all inside, he gets the tools from the back of his truck and hauls them inside the house.

As you steep your tea bag, you give him the plans on yellowing onionskin paper that could have wrapped a child's birthday present a century ago.

"This is it?" He wipes his nose with his sleeve.

"That's it."

"You know I wish I could have taught you how to work with your hands."

"I wasn't . . . really interested."

"No, but . . . I still felt like I failed you in some way. As a father."

"Come on, I think it might be better if we focus on what's in front of us at this moment."

He rolls his tongue around his mouth. After a long pause, he nods. He begins working on the project: a wooden structure inside the room about the size of an outhouse, with a small pinprick the size of a pupil on the wall closest to the window.

The snow has stopped.

Everyone has a passion for something. Some are more visible than others. Some people decide they hate liberals, or conservatives; some people fall in love with Disney movies, or Coca-Cola collectibles; some people decide they want to tie up willing partners with thick ropes and hang them from ceiling hooks and let them turn like Calder mobiles, a slight draft coming from the slightly ajar door rocking their ever-straining forms; some people like craft beers; some people like science fiction; some people decide to appreciate the whimsy of funny neckties; some people consume 90% of their food in a fifty-mile radius around their house. There's a lifestyle of thought and habit for everybody. No one is left behind anymore. For you, as you settle into night, you have decided you want to see your son again, and so you are building the structure, to the specifications you received in the dream, and also the mail—but it was only in the dream that you turned into a slender whale with tiny arms and legs and skirted into an underwater cave with glittering gneiss and schist all around you, cold corals and upside-down icicles, until you surfaced on the other end of the tunnel into a basilica-sized cave, floored with smooth limestone with the small wooden cube at its center. Its surface was painted with arrows and waves. Sliding into air, you were yourself again, as much as you could have been in a dream. Your blowhole crusted over, and your arms and legs lengthened in the dream. Your strawberry blond hair was rooted to your scalp in this dream, and your hips had widened in this dream, and your breasts became full, and the estrogen in your body in the dream felt like molten diamonds. The dream was rife with essentialism but you didn't care, and your father was not in this dream.

But this dream, and what you will build from this dream, isn't about you. This dream is about your son. Inside this dream, you opened the small building's door inside the cave and closed it behind you. The only light was from a pinprick hole on one wall. A faint projection of the cave outside on the wall opposite the pinprick. Upside-down, as with any camera obscura, any projection of light. You put your finger on the edge of the tiny hole and spiraled around it. You dispensed and applied the color of Etruscan Sugar from your finger in the dream, and you began to fill in the spiral with the color as your heart, which for so long you had been uncompromisingly ashamed of, gladdened. Here was where you woke up, shaken by the body you returned to.

As you look out on the sales associate dutifully building the camera obscura with the same rigid cadence your father had before he died, you know what you will do when it is done. After painting the inside of the shed with Etruscan Sugar—the color of lacquered terracotta figurines and hillsides of burning Umbrian wheat—you will watch the wall opposite the pinprick as an image takes shape, even though it will be eight at night when he finishes and the only light outside will be from the streetlights. Watch the image, a bit blurry, but sharp enough, the image of your son in a middle school gymnasium, the clock on the wall saying eight sharp above him and all the dozens of other boys in Cub Scout uniforms with their Pinewood Derby cars, racing them down inclines four apiece. You see your ex-wife with her back to you, in the bleachers, looking back and forth from her phone to your son, but you do not blame her, secretly you would have been bored to tears as well, in an ideal world where you were a regular parent, a regular father—but you also would have been terrified, because of your own Pinewood Derbies of your Cub Scout days, when you were utterly lost and shy and with the boxiest and least aerodynamic Pinewood Derby car possible. Your son's own car, painted brilliant turquoise, is certainly going to do better than yours, thanks to the help of your ex-wife's boyfriend, a carpenter. They live three states away. You could have fought them leaving your city but you were too exhausted and cowed, and the regret has never left you. The scoutmaster takes your son's turquoise car in his hands, and your son looks anxiously about. You miss him so much. You miss how smart he is, and how kind he was to you when he first saw you wearing a wig and lipstick, and you even miss his tantrums. His car is placed at the top of the incline with three others, narrow like pine shivs, and he looks for his mother in the bleachers, scanning around with his hand on his forehead like a sailor searching for land, but his gaze stops, he bites his lip, and his eyes widen, and anyone who happens to be looking at him in that gymnasium would wonder at the absent-minded boy who is staring at a point about seven feet up in the air in the center of the room. He stares, you stare. You smile, you cannot tell whether he has any sense of you, any notion that you are there, until he holds his hand up and waves a little. A tiny wave. He straightens his hair right after waving and turns around, and the scout-master releases the latches keeping the cars, for a little while, from plummeting.

As you might imagine, it's hard to keep in mind that circumstances in the past for you might have been more hellish than circumstances in the present.

Young women stand behind you in the line at Starbucks in one of the downtown skyscrapers. College age, or a bit older. Still living at home during a series of internships, you figure. They're glancing nervously at you, or else you're imagining it. Their skirts and jackets are perfect, and their skin is clear clear clear, free of blemishes, and yours is not, your foundation is the wrong shade because you were too afraid to ask for a color check, and

Arid little everythings, thoughts. You're infuriated that you succumb to them.

As you get your iced coffee and three caramel macchiatos that, honestly, you can't afford, you wonder if this triad of women has ever experienced love. Probably an onrushing tide of it, sweeping over Minnetonka, or Eden Prairie, or whatever exurb they grew up in, with men they met at the yacht club. Let them go, you say to yourself.

No, seriously, let them fucking *go*.

Knockoff purse on your shoulder. A comforting weight stitched together with the same machines in the same factories as the non-knockoff. Comforting pharmacology flowing through your body. Pixie's pills dissolve in your stomach, denying testosterone its lien. Naiad's estrogen patch on the stomach muscle, alternating left and right twice a week. The estrogen allows you to be aware of love, and/or its absence. Some people have thought during your transition that you're a *knockoff*, an off-brand woman, dents and scratches, all sales final.

The deep slowness of a pencil skirt writes your name.

You descend the escalators of the half-dead department store adjoining the Starbucks, juggling the cardboard drink carrier that might sag and collapse at any given moment, ignoring the panhandler at the top. You don't feel particularly good about yourself about that. You know that the panhandler is giving the security guard working the floor part of the cut. For all you know, they might be staying at the same shelter. One half of the floor sells toy AR-15s and bulletproof *Frozen* backpacks, the other sells real guns and lightweight body armor that can fit snugly underneath a polo shirt.

On street level. You sip your iced coffee. The street is mostly empty except for surplus-green tents in the greenway and armed guards in front of the luxury towers. The creative class needs tactical teams to protect them from people who are not them. The black glass of the towers and the black glass of the soldiers' visors create a feedback loop, a cordon around each entrance to the building on the sidewalk, so when they glare at you, you step into the street. They glare at everyone, though. They're not reading you as trans but rather as poor—or if not quite poor-poor, poor enough. Too poor to enter the tower. Their badges are obscured, by design.

Behind the nameplates of the residence towers, you can see the labelscars of the retailers who used to be there on the first floor.

Things have gotten worse behind your back while you were dealing with your own shit. Is it really happening, though? It appears to be, so it must be.

You want to be back in your apartment and the camera obscura, but you have a journey to make. Your half-revealed legs have all these boy scars—nicks from mosquito bites earned camping with your son a few years ago. You scratched them mercilessly, and they never fully healed, right on the diaphanous skin of the shin bone, a little father-and-son bonding time, but even then he knew your heart wasn't quite in it—not with parenting, really, but the whole orchestration of camping out, drowning in an air-sea of mosquitos, erecting a lopsided tent, eating granola bars for dinner since you forgot the hot dogs at home. You constantly scanned your son's face for disappointment, but if he had any, he hid it well, which shouldn't have been anything an eight-year-old had to worry about. Only after the loss of your son in the divorce, of custody, of everyday contact, has the pain really dawned on you, and you know now that your parenting could have been better, more resolute, because you love him, you love him, you love him.

You are not a broken canvas.

Beginning in the fifteenth century, up until the eighteenth or so, some people became afflicted with the delusion that they were made out of glass and would shatter at the slightest touch. This condition appeared in Burton's *Anatomy of Melancholy*, and was later speculated to be a response—of whatever sort—to the development and more widespread use of transparent glass in European cities. King Charles VI of France wore velvet gloves at all times because he was afraid his hands would break into shards. He wore iron rods inside of his clothes. He wasn't afraid of the pieces themselves but of being consumed by the light. Court physicians were at a loss. When he began his reign he was known as *Charles the Beloved* but by the end of his reign he was known as *Charles the Mad*. Each shard was like a memory of the future. This is what light is. You let all the light in, and darkness trembles.

*

You worry that nothing fits you right: worn-out costume jewelry, scuffed consignment flats, red blazers that were a bit too big or small. But in the end they were all bits of cotton and rayon and thin metal clasps and imitation leather. If it's old and worn-down—a little like you—then better than something new, right out of the garment factory. You're just looking for something that will hang from your shoulders and not broaden them, and shoes that help you sway but not look too tall, too apparent.

No stares in the parking garage. Relief. You finish your iced coffee and drive south to Lake Minnetonka, the carrier with the macchiatos riding in the front seat like an uneasy hitchhiker. Hot day. Metal shavings pepper the windshield of your car. You have no idea where they're coming from. Could be from the vast manta ray drones that hover above the plains states. Could be. You're out of windshield fluid so the blades scrape dryly over the curved glass. You probably should call your mother when you get back home.

Your transition, your life as a trans woman, has allowed you to consider time differently than you had before. Every day you are one day closer to death. And yet, each day you transition, you become more fully who you are. Cell by cell. Your cells would be changing anyway, but now they change with a purposeful sweep that becomes more known to you than it would have been otherwise, had you hid away and held back, to choose to solder the mask on your face—it wouldn't have worked anyway, because the mask would be flecking off, bit by bit, losing its adhesion, like a Band-Aid in a swimming pool. You would still have been changing, yet you would have to pretend you were not changing at all, except in the acquisition of stupid hobbies designed to distract you from the ashen necromancy of your unhappy days, your slump, the sounds of terror you'd hear in all other voices, even the dead ones, like your father's.

Time is a train going one way, and your transitioning body another. They both sound off. Two whistles receding from each other. Of course time will circle back around, but you don't have to keep that top-of-mind. When you study the minute changes in your body, time slows for you. And the slowness helps you accept your aging, your forty-three-year-old body, even on those days when you're livid and red-faced and silent at twenty-two-year-old trans women who complain, forlorn, that it's "already too late for them." They are terrified as well, so you try to force grace to inhabit you. Your changes are betting against time, and how you will live before you are laid to rest, when all the hormones in your body will dry up, just as they will in every other human being. You want to be buried in a pine box underneath a beech tree, to decay in the service of something that will grow.

*

As you drive west out of the city, you drive parallel to the hospital trains, one car after another acting as a trauma unit, coursing through the heartland, but you don't know where they are going.

There is a tent city on an abandoned restaurant parking lot along Lake Minnetonka, near what used to be a public dock, one of the only spaces allowed as a "campground" along the otherwise militarized lake shore. It's a lake full of nooks and secrets and cosmetologists' and power lawyers' and commissars' mansions, and inlets, and islands surrounded by designer barbed wire, stained with a lacquer to make the perimeter look like thorned ivory. You don't feel safe anywhere near Lake Minnetonka. The yachts have been converted to gunboats—some painted the color of the Gadsden Flag, some painted the color of the black American flag with the thin blue line in the middle, the American flag of death.

You park in front of a dentist's office that's been converted into a Red Cross station and hike to the camp, balancing the caramel macchiatos under your arm, trying not to look *too* conspicuous. You were told in the email that if anyone gave you trouble to say that you were delivering these for Emoji—and, honestly, you were told (with a grim sincerity that bled from your screen when you read it on your phone), everyone should know anyway. They won't ask you. They'll know.

The air smells like fried meats and diesel. You reach the broken boardwalk and head into the camp, in your white blouse and pencil skirt and black boots with sensible heels.

You want to be an unimaginable mystery for someone.

Again—have things really gone that bad, so quickly, under your nose, without you noticing? You blink. Try to blink the spots away in your eyes from the sun. The past overlaps with the future; usually in the present you can't see the stitches. But they're tearing. A lot of days when you're drained you wish you couldn't. Your struggle has been to get yourself set before the axe really comes down. To erase your past as much as possible. It might not be possible.

Here: a campfire with children huddled around it, roasting pigeons or sparrows or robins, and marshmallows, on sticks. Here is the breakwall and the teenagers jumping from it, shouting and laughing, into the water. Here is the kiosk board with the map of Minnesota with the pushpins where everyone's from. Here they are from Duluth and Rosemount and Northfield and Cosmos and New Ulm and Little Canada. Here are the people who work inside the various compounds and gated communities around Lake Minnetonka, cleaning and gardening and cooking and changing diapers. They are Hmong, they are Somali, they are from everywhere. Here is Little Frogtown, here is Little Little Mogadishu, here is Little Powderhorn, Tibetan prayer flags flapping on tentpoles.

Every day a bus drives by the campground and drops them off at their suburban checkpoints. Usually the bus fare is taken out of wages.

Emoji's tent is unmistakable. It's like a four-person circus tent, purple sashes at the zip-up door. Before you've figured out how to knock, someone calls for you to come in.

When you were thirteen, your Boy Scout troop took an excursion to Florida, the bus full of pork rind bags and off-brand pop cans and sleeping bags. What you loved most was one of the famous lagoons with the crystalline water and the glass-bottom boats. You were the farthest from home you'd ever been and scared quite often, but that was ameliorated for a few minutes on that glass-bottom boat, seeing far below what you thought couldn't be seen before, because the Great Lake water you grew up with was always murky and unknowable. You got down on your hands and knees on the boat, getting the knees of your Scout uniform regulation khakis wet, and you peered down telescopically while everyone around you was punching each other and not paying attention to anything. But you were paying attention to the bottom of the lagoon. There were fish down there, of course, prismatic finned, darting and swimming right underneath the lurching glass-bottomed boat, and you felt yourself to be swimming too. Down there were also cars, really old cars, from a time when people used to drive cars into pristine lagoons and just walk away, when people—no, men—used to leave their families behind and start new lives in new towns without a word or postcard. You didn't know the names of the cars, maybe Studebakers. Then the other Boy Scouts in your troop started laughing at you and calling you a faggot, and you wake up, shuddering, screaming, and Emoji gives you tea. They are sipping their caramel macchiatos, and their cohabitors are sipping theirs.

You gather your breath. The three young women from the coffee shop also huddle there, sipping their frappes. They smile at you, and you manage to smile back. You can't quite fathom the tent. At times it's like a tiny pup tent and at other times its folds and edges stretch beyond your sight. The tea is bitter, and you clench the cup. "How long have I been here?" you ask Emoji, who's sitting cross-legged next to you. *Couple hours. Your own accord.* She shakes her head. *You don't have to do a thing. You can rest.*

It's hard for you to let people in. Acutely aware of this. You wonder if Emoji isn't really here but rather more of an . . . aspirational incarnation. You heard about Emoji from a local trans Facebook group that shut down a few weeks ago because of trolls. A DM from an acquaintance mentioned that the trolls are bankrolled by the Department of Homeland Security.

Emoji changed my life and they will change yours, one of your other acquaintances said. *But don't let*

*anyone else know. The people that want to throw things
at us and kill us can't know.*
All right.

"Do you know if it's possible to transmit dreams from
one person to another?" you ask them. They don't
answer. That is one you'll have to figure out for yourself.
Look at my face, Emoji says. You look at their face.
It's hard to get coffee here, Emoji says. *This is just a
free consultation. What I do is—* They hold a needle-
like instrument, made of a substance that might be bone
might be wood, toward your face, carved with tight spi-
rals. *Laser hair removal and electrolysis burn and zap
out, respectively, the individual hair follicles. They are
extremely painful procedures. You want your skin to
be smooth like glass, I suppose.* You have your first laser
hair appointment in a week. "I never thought that such
a thing was possible. Perfection, I mean." *Good, good,*
Emoji says. *It's possible, but requires thousands of dollars and hundreds of sessions over many years. But
we are not here to talk about your five o'clock shadow.
What I do is . . . a kind of electrolysis for trauma. You
cut it as close to your skin as you can, and then I burn
it out.*

Here are Emoji and their assistants in a conference
room in a Hilton Garden Inn along the highway, remov-
ing esoteric novels and unguents from duffel bags before
their workshop on self-care begins. Here they are along
the breakwall along Lake Minnetonka, soaking their

feet and drinking blue curaçao. Here they are guarding a women's restroom while another trans woman uses it. She's terrified at first, but then relaxes knowing that Emoji won't let any trouble through the threshold. You know that you'll never see them again—not out of malice, but because they need to help a shitload of people, all around the world.

So—again. And again again.

You take a deep breath and tell Emoji that you don't think your trauma necessitates expulsion, or the emotional labor that it would take to extract the trauma. That you can figure it out with the tools at your disposal and also perhaps a good therapist who doesn't try to problematize your gender. You can't quite believe you're saying this. You wanted a *cure* for your pain, but listening to Emoji, you realize that you have the wherewithal to bear it. Not as a performative sacrifice or a noble, suffering queer that others can gaze at from afar, but rather as the seedbed for everything you don't know yet about yourself, but want to, which is a lot.

Emoji nods. *Because you have not been shot for being transgender by a boyfriend, or had a baseball bat in the hands of an uncle crush your ribs?* You nod. *Because you have not been kicked out of your house by your parents?* You nod. *Because you haven't had all ties severed to your child?* You nod and quickly shake your head. "Okay, well, *that's* happened. That's happening." Though that doesn't involve one traumatic event but rather it's like the moon affecting tides, far away and yet with an inexorable gravitational pull. *Hmm. You understand, though. You understand. It's not for everybody. It's not a perfect solution. Nothing is. The extraction itself is painful, and though the trauma will be gone, its absence is palpable. You recommend working to see your son. Doing that work. This group, [ ], can help.* They wrote a name and an email address on a tiny slip of paper and handed it to you. *Though you might have already encountered them already without knowing, with your camera obscura.* Emoji pauses. *It's more of a secret society, truth be told. I prefer to work alone.*

You start driving home, leaving the camp behind, feeling like you made an important decision as yet unclear to you. The sun sets over Lake Minnetonka behind you. You hear small-arms fire from the boats upon the lake. You have a queen-size mattress on the floor and a cat named Smuggler waiting for you inside of the one-bedroom apartment. When you get home you'll remove your makeup with a little cotton cloud. You'll prop your wig up a little so you don't get the astringent on your bangs, and it will make your forehead look huge and like something's wrong with your scalp and hairline. Sometimes you wonder what would happen if you just go out like that, with your wig not right, and see what would happen. If you would break. If the light would still come in.

You and your son are camping along the shore of the lagoon. You are yourself, and the mosquitos are flying mini-figurines of glass insects. Bombardiers. They try to bite you but they can't break your skin, and you and your son laugh and gently wave them off. The glass-bottom boat is in the middle of the lagoon. You and your son decide to walk to it. The dusk is quiet. Your son takes your hand. You think he's feeling serious and sad, but then he skips ahead, dragging you forward and laughing. You laugh too and walk on the surface of the lagoon. Boulders fly off your shoulders, light as balloons. When you reach the glass-bottom boat, it's empty. No Boy Scouts, no other passengers. The boat's mired in the glass surface of the lake like it's ice. Your son hoots and climbs in. You look down through the glass bottom at the Studebakers. They're still there, abandoned.

You wonder whether you'll tell him about what happened here.

When you finally get home, you put your *Shorter Oxford English Dictionary* on Craigslist for $60 o.b.o. The money from selling that two-volume 1,500-page behemoth will go straight into your fund for laser hair therapy for your cheekbones, where you will be burned clean by the entirety of modern English.

You tried writing a semi-autobiographical novel about fifteen years ago. It was a complete novel, with a beginning, middle, and end, so that was something. It was—is, you suppose—called *Forget Me Maybe*. It's a pretty cute title, very 2001, or at least what you considered 2001 to be when it was actually 2001.

It's lost on a floppy disk somewhere at the bottom of one of your storage bins.

Nothing happened in it plot-wise, which might have been forgivable, especially in a first novel, except that you tried to pretend that more-than-nothing happened. Its stabs at poignancy were also coupled with the herky-jerky rhythms of "stuff happening" with no real arc. You figured you were in your late twenties, and a white male, and could get away with it. Many others did.

Stuff that happened to your late-twenties, cis male, copy-editing protagonist included finding an arcade console full of bees, having a friend completely disappear for no reason at all, dating a woman who was pretending to be a fundamentalist Christian, thoroughly exploring an extended dream that took place on the moon, bonding with an old man called the King of Coke-dale who raised llamas in an inner-ring suburb and who later died, and investigating the art of memory palaces, with many discursions of such therein.

Of course, this was a novel of 2001 in a "9/10" sense, not in a "9/11" sense. You heard a lot of security experts and politicians on TV in the ensuing decade use the phrase "a 9/10 mindset." When you finished the first draft in August of that year, you had no idea that this zaniness would be seen as useless, rococo ornamentation—perhaps even a moral affront—even for a young male author. The novel wasn't good, though it was adequate. But the timing, needless to say, was way off, as it probably was for lots of other first-time white, male American novel-ists in their late-twenties who finished their first novels in August of 2001 and still felt very strongly that they had something to say. It was probably for the best that nobody ended up hearing it.

This was a few years before you began cross-dressing in earnest, before you even knew that you had inner com-ponents and as yet unspeakable desires that you needed to let run wild, and then pen up and starve. A cadence you'd repeat over and over again, like you were writing a villanelle with your life. You would collect black boots and underwear and sundresses in Hefty bags, hidden in the trunk of your car, and eventually you would throw them away, and the cycle would start over again. You were always the worse for wear.

At that time, you liked writing about conspiracies. It was absolutely the easy way out to have a shadowy cabal become the root of a narrative's conflict. For example, in *Forget Me Maybe,* a faceless group fueled much of the action to which the protagonist had to react: they placed those magical bees inside an arcade console, they acted as an intermediary between the main character and the King of Cokedale when the King of Cokedale wanted to speak to him, etc., etc. Probably this was the reason the novel ultimately failed. The young male you wanted to get bonus points for showing only select strands of a web of shadows, hinting at a depth and menace that wasn't actually anywhere.

Before you stopped writing altogether, you'd have to say that about two-thirds of your fiction had a conspiracy, almost always supernatural, at the heart of the conflict. Sometimes it worked: you're sure there are, after all, cabals of all sorts that try to determine the course of global events. But these are usually, in real life, much more prosaic than fanciful. The most lurid conspiracies (and cults, you mustn't forget cults) rarely exist in anything more than the imagination.

The people who would like to take away your hormones and revert your birth certificate back to male and kill you believe strongly in conspiracies in which they are the victims, the aggrieved party.

You hope you have escaped those novels.
Your old body was inside those novels.

You and Kierney cut through the parking lot of the Dairy Queen in your Prius to get to the bar where you won't get beat up or killed. Several men in pickup trucks occupy the asphalt veldt of the Dairy Queen parking lot, which the bar shares—they're contractors smoking cigarettes and eating burgers and flicking through contacts on their phones, trying to arrange days uninterrupted by human contact. Daymoon creeps over the highway and the strip mall. Your trip to Lake Minnetonka is beginning to feel faint as you settle back into your usual routine. You know it happened—you don't doubt that—but the edges of your memory of such a dystopia become softer.

You've known Kierney for a long time. She's different from you. Quite. But she's your friend. You're not some kind of hermit.

"_____, let me tell you: when men show pictures of the fish they catch, they're never fucking happier." Kierney puts her leg up on the seat and presses her head against the window. There are selfies you took that morning in your gold sundress—making sure you are at the right angle, arm outstretched, natural smile, not too forced—that you send to men who want the pictures, if not you. These efforts rarely come to much. Messages in bottles, your sundress and your smile, bounce off satellites and into another phone and are deleted.

You've met men at this very bar, but you won't tonight. Last night before you slept when you texted Kierney about Emoji and the camera obscura—which let you glimpse your son—she told you that she had met another trans woman at the bar the other week who had a similar story. And Kierney has a hunch that she'll be there again. You look at the address on the envelope and it seems to match the address of the bar, even though you didn't recall this happening before.

The problem arises because of the fact that you despise this bar.

When Kierney is in the bathroom, you prop yourself up on the bar stool, trying to see who's noticing you, which doesn't seem to be anyone. Fitful with loneliness, you go back to your phone. You have difficulty not checking your email. A few years ago—certainly when you were writing your adequate novel—you found the idea of even having a mobile phone horrifying, and you looked down upon those who constantly had their phone in their clutches, who spoke into it on the sidewalks, in restrooms, in airplanes. Things are very different now and you have, in a sense, lost. Everyone has lost. You have been grafted onto the phone like a chrysanthemum onto a wormwood stalk, your brain extending invisibly up to the satellites.

Applications spring out of the plastic and rare earth minerals and the hard plastic coffin casing enclosing the phone to prevent shattering: email, weather, voicemails, your bank account, your Starbucks account, Instagram, Audible, a flashlight, music, Kindle, Facebook, iTarotLite, Find Phone, Kik, Safari, and a trio of dating apps that you've been known to call the *unholy trinity* when you're more than a little drunk. The ones who sent you the plans in the mail have to be the same ones who had sent you the dream. Or it could have just been one person. Your freelance inbox is empty. You look up "wolf whale" on Google Images and come across the earliest ancestor of whales, which was a wolf, or a kind of wolf-hippopotamus. So that's who you were in the underwater cave. It's possible at least.

You think it might not be terrible, finding someone to love, but you have no idea how to go about it. Truly.

You read on your phone: *What people wear to get into Kierkegaard, the world's most exclusive night-club.* It's in Dubai, or Dublin—Kierney sits down next to you. Actually you didn't arrive at the bar with your friend Kierney, you don't have a friend Kierney. You drove there yourself and passed the men in their pickup trucks with Home Depot supplies in the cab as they eat their burgers and smoke. The Dairy Queen parking lot is full so you have to park on the street. You keep your head up as you walk. You don't want to seem like an easy target.

Kierney hasn't gone to the bathroom, because she doesn't exist, but you do sit at the bar by yourself, elbows on the zinc, the bar that you don't particularly like, and think about wolf-whales, and the size of your breasts, and whether you can get up to a B-cup with the estrogen, and Dutch still lifes.

A dream: you are with your ex-wife and son in a car driving on a low bridge across a massive glassy lake. You are still married to your ex-wife in the dream. Your son is strapped into his car seat in the back. A wave comes—both sides, white, white foam, surf—and it takes the car. Your son and ex scream. You are sure you're all going to drown. The car will take water, you're sure of it. The water surges over the windshield. The wheels jostle. You want to protect them, but there doesn't seem to be any way this is possible.

But the car somehow holds, and the car is still on the bridge. Your ex and son are silent. They're disappointed, you realize as they stare at you, because you didn't let them drown.

Far below in the water, fins.

How many times can you revise yourself? Too many incomplete thoughts swim through your head. Maybe all of this would be easier if you were able to speak them out loud with a friend, in a dialogue.

"As you know, _____," Kierney says, "you might be in the same boat as other trans people who *didn't* know at a super young age that they were trans. That they were *different*. You know, the story you hear all the time. But your experiences are valid too!"

"Right," you say winningly, taking a sip of your Grain Belt Premium, and take a look around the LGBT-friendly dive bar, which doesn't seem so bad to you after all, for a few seconds! "That's the standard narrative. And there's nothing wrong with that narrative. You have plenty of trans acquaintances who have expressed such a story."

"And I'm one of them!" Kierney says, looking around the bar to see who is watching you. This bar dates from the 1920s, but not in an interesting or vintage way. It's just old. There's a tiny and sad dance floor which no one ever dances on. And a surly male bartender who calls you "honey" mournfully every time you order and tells you to move away from the center of the bar, which is supposed to be kept clear of people, or something, even though there's a bar stool right in front of the "go zone," and moreover makes a big deal about checking your ID every time "since he doesn't know you." And there's a pool table, you guess. In late afternoon there's almost no one here. A crunchy-looking lesbian couple in their fifties sits at a side table. A man wearing a black cape—is there a convention in town?—plays darts. On busy nights when you contend with crowds there are also many more trans people, mostly other trans women, or cross-dressers, as this bar is one of the few "safe" places of expressivity in the metro area. But you hate that this is the case, that this dive bar is the default space, the normative experience that you, if you are trans, are supposed to suck up and enjoy—the horrible lighting that makes your makeup look caked on, the aforementioned despondent barkeep, and of course the chasers, the male fetishists who frequent the bar for the promise of fantasy sex with trans women. You suspect that this bar's rather low, faux-gilt ceiling is the limit to a trans person's love for far too many men, men who are too ashamed to meet you anywhere else, to take you out to a restaurant like any other normal fucking woman. But you have been ashamed, too, because of your loneliness, for taking men up on their own mediocrity, for meeting them halfway if not more, and making out with them in the corner of the bar near the pool table here, or letting a man's hand creep up your skirt under the table and rub your panties here, or finding a corner of the parking lot in your car on the other side of the Dairy Queen, where it is always dark, and masturbate each other. The first time you touched a penis beside your own, he came on your pencil skirt twenty seconds later, and his head jolted around quickly when the headlights of a car swam across his face like the light from a Coast Guard patrol boat searching for drug runners along the breakers, and he pulled your sticky hand away, though the car kept searching for a parking spot elsewhere, and he said *I'm married* and you said *all right*, your heart sinking. You cleaned the semen off your skirt with a towelette from your glove compartment and he went back to his own car, which he parked a couple blocks away.

"You still here, _____?" Kierney asks, snapping her fingers in front of your face and laughing.

"Are you?" you ask.

"Hmm, not really," she says, taking a last brave draught of her watery Cosmopolitan. "But listen, I hear you. It can be hard to navigate what other trans people are going through, their own stories crowding out your own. You're so desperate for validation that you let yourself writhe around the jealousy for a little bit, just because it holds a tiny bit of hope as well." She pauses and levels her eyes at you. "This will happen to you one day, you know. Someone will look up to you. You and your transition."

"What?" you say, finishing the bottle. "No. No way."

For many years, you had tried so hard to build a closet to live within. You've tried to create meaning from those years, when you were cross-dressing and considered yourself little more than a shameful secret that happened to have a body. Kierney seems to be reflecting back to you. You do have other friends, other people who care about you, even though you don't see them as often as you like. But you didn't want to bring them here into this bar with you, on a fool's errand to find a dream transmitter.

"No, it's true," Kierney says. "And what will you possibly do with yourself when that happens?"

"Well," you say. "I suppose that will be a moment to reflect on my growth."

Kierney laughs.

"How did you know that you were a girl at such a young age?" you say, trying for once to initiate a conversation with Kierney.

"The usual suspects," she says, shrugging. "Wanting to play with Barbies instead of Tonka trucks. Trying on my sister's dresses instead of playing football with the other boys. My parents thought that I was gay. I thought I was gay." She shook her head. "There were just no words available—to me, to any of us—to describe what I was going through. *The words could not be conceived.* It was only in college that I heard about transgender people even existing, even if it was self-evident that they were to be despised. Well, listen to me, I'm dominating the conversation."

"No you're not," you say. You turn to see a woman in a burly coat, head down, wide-brimmed hat, bursting through the door and walking as the crow flies to the back room, a parlor of sorts where karaoke takes place on weekends but which is now dark and closed. She opens it and shuts it behind her. And it might not have been a woman after all. Indeterminate. The person smelled like lavender. You turn back to Kierney to tell her that you never started dating men until after you had fully come out, and that your attraction to men had been buried under layers and layers of anxiety and self-directed homophobia, to the point where it never registered within your waking life—but Kierney is gone.

You are not as surprised as you thought you'd be.

When you first began your journey, other trans women sometimes angered you. You knew, deep down, that their lives were fraught with the usual unusual perils—rejection, staggering loss of friends and family, wending role inversions, the like—but still you looked at the surfaces they'd created and became filled with envy and embarrassment about your own middling station. You judged those who wanted to fade into the tapestry of womanhood and leave behind everything else, like a thief sneaking into an eternal palace (by *stealth)* and who has no plans to return with her treasures and scale the walls back again into the cool moonlit mandrake night, to leave the palace floating and stretching/sketching itself as far as the eye can see, for of course the treasures are hers to begin with, it's true—lip gloss, corset, spirolacatone, hierantiphallatin, sarxion compounds packed in the funerary urns of minor princesses, day-glow sticks from endless parties to be roasted over fire pits and eaten in the company of jailers, tanners, hairdressers and assorted stylists, and assembly line workers at sex toy factories. In this palace one can go forever down hallways, banquet halls, master bedrooms, guest bedrooms, helot bedrooms, inner dwarf gardens . . . In this palace it becomes much more sensible to stop being a thief and join the household staff who serve a queen none of the other women have ever seen. And there might be two to two hundred queens anyway—impossible to tell who's really in charge. So no one's in charge, which makes it easier to live there.

These are the women who sometimes consider the fact they were born as male as a "glitch," a correctable error. Does a proofreader pine over old mistakes corrected? Never! So they plan for surgery, get surgery, disappear. You'll never see them at your little support group ever again.

Yes, of course I'll call you!

This would absolutely *break* you. You thought you were all in it together.

There were portents of your womanhood, sure. Signs that went beyond your own shame that only became achingly clear in retrospect. Like when you'd see a trans woman in a supermarket or coffee shop and think, without a hint of self-reflection, *That can never be me. Their lives must be so hard.*

Of course there were.

When you were twenty-three, a woman in your MFA program kissed your inner thigh on the kitchen floor of your efficiency and told you that she liked that part of you the most, because it was most like a woman's— and though you were secretly thrilled you had no way to know what it meant.

Your femur, however, volted.

You had no idea what to do with that moment. The electricity had nowhere to go.

When you were thirty-three during a weekend at your ex's family cabin, a female friend painted your toenails rose-gold on a whim. You were giddy, even when the paint began to chip and fade.

You never considered, though, recreating that feeling by painting your toenails yourself.

You get up from the stool, the bartender squinting at you as he dries mugs with a washcloth, and stride toward the back room.

"Honey," says the bartender behind you, "you can't go in there."

You ignore him, resisting the urge to say something cutting, and throw open the door. It takes a while for your eyes to adjust, but it's not quite the space you remember from a previous sullen and drunken karaoke night. It's more of a Viking longhall. A massive fireplace blazes along the far wall. Rough-hewn wooden tables. When you reach back to close the door behind you, the knob is carved as a medusa's head.

The person you followed sits alongside the fireplace, warming their hands and shivering. You sit next to them. Emoji had seemed to live in the future, and this person seems to live in the past.

"Excuse me," you say quietly, "but do you know—"

They hold up a hand. They seem to be listening for something.

You wait for a good minute, and then you're going to say more, you are impatient, but they interrupt your non-silent silence.

"Yeah, we've helped you," they say. It's hard for you to get a read on their face, or their mannerisms for that matter. "And we'll keep helping you, on occasion. You need to be kinder to yourself."

"Who's 'we'?"

"There are lots of wes."

"Hmm." The heat from the fireplace is bearable, but only just so. In the distance, someone's singing a sea shanty.

"The camera obscura—is that helping?"

Suddenly it makes sense. This small part, at least. "Those plans were from you?"

A slight nod.

"Yes. Yes! Thank you. It's . . . it's good to see my son every once in awhile."

"Most of our work is for others who happen to be in more dire straits than you are. But that doesn't mean you, and others losing hope while caught in the skein of late American capitalism, don't deserve help as well. Just . . . a little less than the trans women who are getting their throats slit."

"Thanks," you say. And you mean it.

They nod. "I have to go. You was only dropping something off. You should be getting back to Kierney." They turn and face you for the first time. "Hold out your hand."

You hold out your hand, and they press a small coin, bluish metal, into your palm. You turn it over and over. On one side is a cherub of sorts, wings outstretched; on the other side is a blue star, and on the third side is written: "ORIOLE."

"Break in case of emergency," the person says. They turn toward the fireplace and slide into its blazing logs.

"Holy shit!" you say, but the person appears to be unharmed. Their clothes don't burn—they don't even smolder. The person stands up inside the fireplace and finds handholds in its chimney, climbing up.

*

You expect a lecture from the bartender, but he doesn't pay you any mind.

"Ready to go?" Kierney says, smiling, tilting her head.

"Sure," you say, taking a deep breath. "Sure."

You look at your watch. Hours have passed. How have hours passed? You remember that your meter has expired. You start running toward it, the impossible coin clutched in your fist, weaving through the trucks in the parking lot, and say, *Shit*.

And right then—though you have idea where it comes from, rising up—you're filled with a sadness that has no meaning, no place, only time. It's like when you were twelve years old, maybe eleven, when you swore for the first time. You'd said swear words before on dares, or in joking, but those didn't really count. No, this was when you swore behind your cousin's back— the cousin who never speaks to you anymore, who steals from your grandmother by living with her and never doing anything for her, not even buying a Christmas card—much less a present—for your eitghty-eight-year old grandmother who's watched his illegitimate children for years for free without thanks, *that* cousin, three years younger than you. The cousin was running away after a joke or a measure of proto-bullying, and you said, *Damn you*. It was a curse from the mouth to the heavens down on the cousin's skull, and swiping the parking ticket off the windshield wiper of your Prius, you realize that that was the last day you were innocent. It was all gone after that. Your cousin's now a cop in your old hometown.

*

There was one time where you thought you were going to die at a man's hands, or his knife, but that is another story, one you are not prepared to dwell on, most days.

"Oh, by the way, there's karaoke Friday at the bar," Kierney says, when you're back in city traffic. She seems to know where she lives, where she has to go. "You up for it?"

You pause for at least a minute. Kierney doesn't seem to mind the silence.

"Yeah," you say.

You vow that every one of your stories will have at least one sliver of emancipation.

It feels indulgent. Like you're going to use all the freedom up.

You call your ex.

"What the hell, it's seven?" Mary says after the third ring.

"Sorry." You hate apologizing to her. "Is Aaron up? I just wanted to say hi."

She sighs. "No, he's at hockey practice."

"Seems a little early."

"How would you know?" she says. When you say nothing—because this call is seeming like an increasingly bad idea, you want to hang up, you're a fool—she says: "Ice time is hard to come by."

"Okay." Panic begins to creep in. "Okay, look—I'm sorry. Just tell him I called and said hi, if you could?"

"I will." In a hesitant but precise tone that imparts upon you that she is saying this against her better judgment, she says: "Look, we can set up a regular time to call or Skype. Does that work? Tonight doesn't work but maybe tomorrow night?"

"Yeah," you say, and you will move mountains for this. "Sounds cool, if he's up for it."

"I think he will be," she says. "I'll text you. Have a good morning, _____."

"You too," you say, and hang up. You hold your iPhone flat in your palm. It's heavy and warm, like a floor tile warmed by geothermal energy. You try to take a deep breath from your belly then go to the bathroom.

Like hundreds of other times before, you stare at your face in the medicine cabinet mirror without your wig and are shocked at how non-feminine you look without it. Not exactly masculine—you give yourself that one kindness—but something else. You wonder about the woman whose hair this wig came from, what compelled her to cut it and sell it and have it enmeshed and reassembled in a Guangzhou wig factory. How it once was part of a growing and changing human being, then was snipped, stored, and bathed in silicon (even the "natural" hair wigs are coated in silicon, to mimic the sheen of a real head of hair). The wig is your most important possession—on most days, you don't feel like you look like a woman without it.

And it jolts you in a tiny way each time you put it on.

Your cat jumps on your vanity. One of her ears is shorter than the other. She knocks over your boar-hair brush.

"Jesus Christ, Smuggler," you say.

As if there's an objective lens to view whether you fully appear (in many eyes) to yourself as female or not, or something in between, when you are not wearing a wig. Footage from a surveillance camera affixed to a bank's ceiling, for example. Or the hidden eye of a portrait painting you don't own, or even have a poster of—some omniscient tulip merchant from Haarlem, perhaps, bourgeois stability from the past. On second thought, a tulip merchant is too exotic, speculative, always on the precipice of ruin in macro-historical terms. A butter merchant then, dairy being a solid trade in any economic times, crash-proof really, resistant to amoral financiers excoriated by the Reformed preachers of Haarlem in the pulpit, along with sodomites, the inebriated, and the English, the gamblers, and the indolent. Likely there was panic about cross-dressing men as well in mid-seventeenth century Holland, ruled under the sign of Calvin and the depravity of all living beings. The eye of this nonexistent painting observing this set piece, this tableau of you wigless lying on your futon widthwise, laptop on your lap, reading Google News in your browser about legal battles in the courts as to whether you have legal personhood or not, makes the grief well up for a few seconds, a familiar form of discomfort, and you close the laptop, go to the bathroom, urinate (about 50/50 chance of you standing up or sitting down), and look at yourself in the mirror, safely out of the view of the nonexistent butter merchant, and think of how your gender can be a painting: utterly still yet following your every motion.

You're so tired. You curl up inside the camera obscura. When you nap in the ancient machine you wonder: if you are going to transition anyway, why can't you transition to a woman in the late seventeenth century? What is to stop you? Why can you not only change the curve of your hips, and the fullness of your breasts, but also time? Sure, it's a bloody era, yes, yes, but to be a woman who makes her own way in a world that hasn't been consumed by floods and droughts in equal measure is a tantalizing prospect, even if you don't fully understand it.

You wish to go there.

Though the esoteric was frowned upon in Holland in the seventeenth century, the craft of mixing one's own paints, or boiling rabbit hairs into a *size* in order to treat a linen canvas also involved imposing one's will upon fragments of the material world.

But becoming a woman isn't quite so programmatic.

And essences can't be as easily distilled. They can't be measured or measured precisely. This was the failure—the desire to stop seeing essences.

You imagine going farther back. When every rock, every drop of water, every fleeing muskrat and bear skull was imbued with spirit, but every thing also devoid of hierarchy. Becoming a woman at that time would involve being like a chickadee, or a poplar tree, or a vein of copper under a mountain.

Having a fixed thing-ness is inexorably tied to fate. Knowing one's place in the world is a sign of what has already been done, even though it hasn't happened yet, or been spoken yet.

You know this is all wrong, at root *inaccurate*, but you want your inaccurate moments.

You want to utterly possess them.

"Hey, Aaron!" you say through your computer to his computer, trying to go for cheerful, relaxed, even though he will be able to hear right through you, oh no. "How's it going?"

"Fine?" He is eleven. His hair is bushy and all over the place and you think of all those times you tousled his hair when he was younger and he was in your life every day, and you had no idea that he would one day not be with you anymore.

Mary mumbles something in the background. You imagine her hissing sotto voce instructions.

"Um, how are you?" he says.

"Oh, pretty good," you say. "Just, you know, working a lot. It's really good to hear your voice."

"Uh huh."

"How's hockey?"

"It's . . . fine?" he says. "I'm a goalie."

"Awesome. Listen, I . . . I'm sorry, Aaron. I wish I was there for you more."

"Yeah, well, you're not," he says, the first thing he's said that doesn't feel vague or put-upon.

"I get that. I really get that."

"You're not," he repeats.

"But maybe we can talk on the phone a little bit more? Do you still play Minecraft?"

"Minecraft?" He sighs. "No, not really. I mostly play Fortnite."

"Oh, cool," you say. "I've never played it but I know a lot of people who do."

"Yeah, mom doesn't really like it." He pauses. He frowns and pushes his hair to the side. He looks like an eleven-year-old trying to hold it together for a parent that he hasn't seen in more than a year. "I don't play that either. I figured it would be the thing that you'd like to hear."

"Wait, what? Aaron, I just want you to be your—"

He hangs up.

Do the one thing that will save you before anything else. Remember—if you can't take care of yourself, how do you expect to care for anyone else?

Any existential question about wigs is precluded by the fact that they can be severely uncomfortable to wear. They itch. But your male-pattern baldness hair, or the remnants of it, despite its mitigation by estrogen (though, on account of your age, not nearly enough as you would like) doesn't make you any less of a woman. Hair—not enough in the right places, too much in the wrong places—can't make you more or less of a woman. In repose or walking, you are a woman. A trans woman, which is accretive with womanhood and not mutually exclusive with it.

There has to be some form of continuity in order to have this story make sense. The camera obscura has to be in your living room. You can touch it. It is there. Definitely there. Emoji has to be alive. She is alive. And you had to have visited them, as well as the messenger in the bar. The late winter air has a cold tang to it that you can taste, and seeps through the cracks of your poorly insulated windows.

You go inside the camera obscura again. The camera obscura—as far as you can remember—was fashioned by Dutch lens-grinders in seventeenth-century Holland. It might have been, at the outset, a way to create illusions for enjoyment rather than as an aid for drawing and painting. They were so close to discovering photography—all that was needed was silver nitrate and paper and salt. In the 1830s when photography was first developed as a commercial project, photographs were known as "photogenic drawings." People out on the street will see you as they want to see you. They will create the image of you that they want and there is nothing you can do to stop it.

Hairs, real or synthetic, dry out, and you look at your phone, go through the motions. It's difficult to concentrate. Difficult to know what to say, to reach out. Your son, you worry, has your same temperament. *Please, anything but that,* thinking of how you have your own father's temperament.

You never let the phone leave your purse.

All of these signals, these atomized packets of hope.

You spend the evening with a pick, untangling snarls and watching *Handmaid's Tale.*

Ode to Psyche
by John Keats
with annotations

O Goddess! hear these tuneless numbers, wrung
By sweet enforcement and remembrance dear,
And pardon that thy secrets should be sung
Even into thine own soft-conched ear:
Surely I dreamt today, or did I see
The winged Psyche with awakened eyes?
I wandered in a forest thoughtlessly,
And, on the sudden, fainting with surprise,
Saw two fair creatures, couched side by side
In deepest grass, beneath the whisp'ring roof
Of leaves and trembled blossoms, where there ran
A brooklet, scarce espied:

*Your dealbreakers for profiles on Tinder you see include
the following:*

Holding a gun
  Holding up a middle finger

Saying they have graduated from the "school of hard knocks" or "Hard Knocks University" in the education info field
"All lives matter"
"Blue lives matter"
"Down to fuck/dtf"
Ending a profile with a comma
Any images that solely consist of skull and cross-bones
Dead or dying flailing gasping fish in outstretched human hands
"Christ follower"
Slain deer
The Confederate flag

'Mid hushed, cool-rooted flowers, fragrant-eyed,
Blue, silver-white, and budded Tyrian,
They lay calm-breathing on the bedded grass;
Their arms embraced, and their pinions too;
Their lips touched not, but had not bade adieu,
As if disjoined by soft-handed slumber,
And ready still past kisses to outnumber
At tender eye-dawn of aurorean love:
The winged boy I knew;
But who wast thou, O happy, happy dove?
His Psyche true!

Most pictures of men on Tinder are taken:

In their car or truck
At a wedding that isn't theirs, usually with a bevy of other high school or college buddies

On a fishing boat
In a restroom of a bar where they're more than a
little drunk and they lean toward the mirror and they're
smiling in anticipation of what this photo will net
In the middle of the woods, flash reddening their
eyes and marrow, grasping antlers like the wheel of a
clipper in the middle of a storm, taking water
Of their cars/motorcycles/boats, with no human in
sight

O latest born and loveliest vision far
Of all Olympus' faded hierarchy!
Fairer than Phoebe's sapphire-regioned star,
Or Vesper, amorous glow-worm of the sky;
Fairer than these, though temple thou hast none,
Nor altar heaped with flowers;
Nor virgin-choir to make delicious moan
Upon the midnight hours;
No voice, no lute, no pipe, no incense sweet
From chain-swung censer teeming;
No shrine, no grove, no oracle, not heat
Of pale-mouthed prophet dreaming.

First messages you've received:
Hey
Hi
Hey beautiful
What's up?
hello Beautiful, what a nice and sparkling face
Good morning darling
Hi Honey. lets party
I like blondies ☺

*Wyd right now id love to cum have some fun . . . I'm
very well endowed*
*Would you mind telling me why you haven't written
me yet?*
I've always wanted to be with a shemale

O brightest! though too late for antique vows,
Too, too late for the fond believing lyre,
When holy were the haunted forest boughs,
Holy the air, the water, and the fire;
Yet even in these days so far retired
From happy pieties, thy lucent fans,
Fluttering among the faint Olympians,
I see, and sing, by my own eyes inspired.
So let me be thy choir, and make a moan
Upon the midnight hours;
Thy voice, thy lute, thy pipe, thy incense sweet
From swinged censer teeming;
Thy shrine, thy grove, thy oracle, thy heat
Of pale-mouthed prophet dreaming.

*Results of dates have included: A secret boyfriend of
the woman you agreed to see tagging along the date,
because they wanted "a threesome with a tranny"*
*A man refusing to open the door to his house or
acknowledging that you were standing on the doorstep for the date, even though you'd texted him twenty
minutes before—he texted an hour later that he had
received a tattoo of a bear earlier that day on his chest
and was in too much pain and much too exhausted to
see anyone and was too embarrassed to actually tell
you this while you were at his doorstep feeling like*

a fool, an utter fool, but he was really sorry and still wanted to see you

Your date eyeing you through the window of the coffee shop and walking away across the street back to his car; you catch him out of the corner of your eye and he thinks you can't see him, but you can see him clearly, in all aspects, and his face says to you that he didn't realize that you were a trans woman, it was too much for him to bear, the fear of being seen with you, a shame palatable, imagining all the stares upon the both of you in the coffee shop and therefore the flirting, kind language he had for you was said in vain, wasted on a woman who wasn't enough of one for him, which made you angry more than anything else; you weren't sad, you forced yourself not to be sad about this unknown man, you would not let him make you sad

Yes, I will be thy priest, and build a fane
In some untrodden region of my mind,
Where branched thoughts, new grown with
    pleasant pain,
Instead of pines shall murmur in the wind:
Far, far around shall those dark-clustered trees
Fledge the wild-ridged mountains steep by steep;
And there by zephyrs, streams, and birds, and
    bees,
The moss-lain dryads shall be lulled to sleep;
And in the midst of this wide quietness
A rosy sanctuary will I dress
With the wreathed trellis of a working brain,
With buds, and bells, and stars without a name,

With all the gardener Fancy e'er could feign,
Who breeding flowers, will never breed the same:
And there shall be for thee all soft delight
That shadowy thought can win,
A bright torch, and a casement open at night,
To let the warm Love in!

II.

Then, darker.
You heard over and over again that the rest of the world had decided a long time ago that trans women didn't deserve love, and that they had to find it from each other. You heard it on NPR in a calm voice: *A new study shows that most people do not consider trans women worthy of love . . . we have brought two experts on the issue to discuss both sides of the story . . .* You saw it in curated push notifications on your phone's notifications. You figured you had to do something regarding what you deserve and didn't deserve. That you had to cast your own die.

When you first started dating you were filled with gratitude, and yet annoyance, when you received any interest whatsoever. That the purpose of dating was to create a temporary union driven by circumstance rather than choice. And fate as well—but a weak sort of fate. Your loneliness convinced you that this was the way to be less alone. You were content but not happy as you went through this process, and yet you failed to see the distinction at the time.

You also wondered whether the fate that would repel or attract you to another person would feel the same:

anxiety at the base of the skull, breathlessness, a slight tinge of annoyance as you flip through profiles on your phone, tired of a solitary queen-size bed.

You forced your heart to open up as if you used the jaws of life to pry apart a crashed car, an accident rather than an orchid.

When you asked Esme out, she was surprised but readily agreed. You'd met her at the biweekly trans support/ social group you went to every once in a while. You saw yourself as a "starter woman." A recently hatched egg foundling foal fawn. You had just recently come out at work, and you still weren't on a full dose of your tit-tacs, taking your transformation slowly and not trying to rush anything. But you felt like a moving target. Esme was a lot more established in who she wanted to be. Understanding other trans women's interiority was surprisingly difficult. You expected better of yourself. Everyone's bodies were in such different stages at those meetings and at the beginning of your transition, you craved the finished states of the more "advanced" trans women, even if they were "wrapping things up" legally or socially. Of course, you thought that most of them were still alone, and you read your own anxieties about fitting in and getting clocked as theirs. How the heart becomes pierced when imagining other people's loneliness.

Esme had curly blond hair. She was maybe three or four years older than you. She lived a quiet life, you thought. Above a coffee shop. You met at a Mediterranean deli.

She joked that she didn't want to meet in the coffee shop below her apartment; it "hit too close to home."

She made dinner for you in that apartment: salad, Merlot, a Portuguese lamb stew. She was so happy and you were a monster, you were such a heartless fucking monster. You decided you needed to leave after you realized she didn't actually pity you. The fact that she treated you like a human being and tried to regard you plainly was almost too much to bear. It was, it was too much bear.

Venus is clearly cis (myrtle, rose, apple, poppy). Venus is vengeful, unknowable (dove, sparrow, swan, hare, goat, ram). Venus cries in her gold-plated bathroom and then sends out threatening texts from it. Venus charms. Venus has soft lines and lens flares. Venus is able to make it up as she goes along. Venus doesn't know why she has it in for Psyche—wait, no, of course she does. Venus lives alongside a rose-gold lake. The people begin to worship Psyche instead of Venus. Venus is jealous! Psyche doesn't want the worship, *please please leave me alone, I just want to transition in peace*, she says. Psyche's father receives a bad oracle from Apollo that Psyche's progeny could very well destroy the world so he decides to kill Psyche, for whom *marriage and death are merged into a single rite of passage*, for the good of the country. *Don't you walk away from me. Show some respect*

They leave Psyche on a rocky crag to die among the elements. This was when the West Wind, the zephyr, was moved to pity for this poor girl on a promontory, and he swept her up into the air, and deposited her in a faraway meadow, a locus amoenus. And she sleeps for a long time, among the sweetgrass and clover.

Venus sighs and tells her son Cupid to take care of the problem. Venus is a girlboss.

Venus soon enough puts Psyche under her thumb.

You made matches, you wrote messages, but you had no means to build interiority through the disinterest of other people. All of the energy you had was harnessed into your transition. It took a lot of work to simply acknowledge that the changes you sought were both necessary and thrilling. In spite of all the constant anxieties about uprooting yourself completely in the world, you were overjoyed. The interiority you had was the one you inherited when you were four and you realized that you could think about tastes but the actual taste would not be there. Now you look for validations. You build interiority on the outside: the slight curve of your breasts is cognition, and the thinning of your arm hair—thin and black to fine and gray—is the resolution of the subconscious.

When you drive home from your evening with Esme, nerves jangled, you see the checkpoints from the National Guard, the Humvees parked in front of the Wendy's.

Time compresses into apple seeds.

You'd thought that nothing was worse than being alone. Nothing.

*

*Find out what happens when the jealous Venus com-
manded her son Cupid (the god of love) to inspire
Psyche with love for the most despicable of men, and
how he fucked it up by stabbing himself with the very
same arrow of fate and passion!*

You went out alone anyway to the dance night at the lesbian bar one Saturday, but Esme couldn't come with you
because she had gotten her hair tangled in a knot and
she couldn't get it out.

You had called a friend to go with you but she backed
out at the last minute.

Anyway, you decide to go out yourself; you scan
the crowd in the middle of the bodies. You wade into
the middle of the crowd. There is a picture of this that the
bar took and put on their website, along with a hundred
others. You are clearly yourself, clearly trans, hip-hop on
the speakers, and staring out, looking for—something?
Someone. Definitely a someone. But who? You felt like
an Amazon, even though you're not particularly tall (for
a trans woman).

If someone flipping through on Facebook saw that
picture, what would they think of you? *Desperate.*

You start dancing but you are still looking, trying to
make eye contact, while fifteen miles away Esme goes to
sleep to Basque folk music on her clock radio.

When you were cross-dressing in secret, you'd hide the
clothes you bought online: in an upper alcove of your
closet, in the compartment of your car's trunk where you

kept the spare tire. You'd stuff everything in a heavy-duty black garbage bag and hope that neighbors or your wife never noticed. You tried to make it out—as justification, if you were ever caught—just recycling, trash, a bunch of clothes to give to Goodwill, not belonging to any certain person. Random fabrics. You purged those black bags more than once, and then after a couple of weeks you would start over again, needing the silk against your skin and the wrinkled dresses hanging from your shoulders even though they wouldn't quite fit your body.

Eventually you got up the courage to shop in Target or JCPenney for women's clothes, and you were certain that everyone in the entire store relentlessly stared at you. You would bring a little piece of paper to make it seem like you were shopping dutifully for your wife—you'd stare down at the paper and squint at the clothes in front of you, all while your heart beat so quickly in your rib cage that you thought you were going to lose your breath. And this was from fear of getting caught and laughed at, yes, fear of getting shamed for having these urges to be in women's clothes in the first place—but you were also beyond thrilled. These fabrics, these cuts, showed you another form and possibility of your life, even if the speedball emotions were too concentrated to truly appreciate these possibilities. It would take years to untangle them, to lay them flat on the bed, to ascertain not only the potential you had to become a woman, but that you already were a woman, and everything else was a papered-over façade that deserved the fire. It's so difficult to live a lie, except when it's been everything you've ever known.

*

As you bob on this sea of days, your mother calls you. You have to steel yourself before you connect. Make sure you are breathing correctly. It's not her fault, you tell yourself. You're taking a walk around a lake. It's late summer this time. The Canadian geese crowd the path, and only veer away at the last second. The goslings, now no longer rumpled, are almost ready to fly.

"Hi, Mom," you say, edging past a puddle on the trail.

"Oh, hi, deadname. Are you busy?" your mother says, coughing. "I never know when to call."

You suck in breath through your teeth. "That's . . . not my name anymore, Mom."

"Oh," she says. "I keep forgetting, deadname. It's just so hard for me to keep track."

It's been four years, you want to tell her. *It's been four years since I told you that I wasn't deadname anymore.*

"How are you?" you manage to say.

"Oh," she says. "You know. It's hard here in the house. It's hard without your father. Just the other day I was having pain in my jaw."

"I understand," you say.

"But how are you?" she says. This surprises you. Before you get to answer: "Are you eating enough?"

"Plenty," you say.

"And your job? You still have a job, right?"

This is more complicated than you are willing to admit. "Yeah, Mom, job is going fine. You know, I'm busy."

"Hmm," she says. "Your cousin came over and mowed the lawn for me, and cleared some brush in the old garden. The one with the Saint Anthony statue. You know that one, right? I'm still praying for you, by the way."

"I know," you say.

"I pray the rosary for you every day. I know you don't like me saying that, deadname, but I am. And I hope your son is still able to go to church."

"I don't know if he is," you say. "You should call Mary." You've wondered, on many occasions, whether your parents thought of Mary as the child they never had—and after you transitioned, whether they doubled down on that assumption. That they could never see you as a daughter. When you announced the divorce they didn't offer support, but instead treated it as an inevitability that was at long last revealed. Because you supposed yourself a woman, in their eyes, you didn't deserve marriage, with your ex or anyone.

"Maybe I will," she says, drifting off.

"Aaron would love to hear from you," you say, assuming a familiarity with what Aaron wanted that was illusory at best.

"What do you know what your grandson wants," your mother says, and you can hear the tears filling up her eyes, and you hang up. There is no more you can take.

One minute later, you call back. "Sorry, Mom, it must have been a bad connection." You pause. "You know these cell phones."

The next date with Esme: *you are horrible at talking, there is a cat outside, mewling on the edge of a dumpster, who is better at communicating, you also hear gunshots from two or three blocks away—*

The bedsheets smell like marjoram, rosemary, like
her kitchen, they smell like the cargo hold of a clipper
ship from the eighteenth century—
  Police sirens, gunshots—
You take off your butterfly panties.
You don't want to fuck her.
"I can't do this, I'm sorry," you say, and in a concussive force you float out of the window backward, over the city, and back into your bedroom, onto your queen mattress.

The last look she gives you is perplexed, but not surprised.

"Fuck!" you say. You open your nightstand and you get the three-sided coin out. You spin it on your palm. You toss it into the drawer and close it shut. ORIOLE.

Many years later, in a seam of the future, you see Esme in a crowd at a neighborhood art fair in the city. She's arm-in-arm with a cis woman and happy. She has tattoos of pirate roses up and down her arms. She doesn't see you. She buys a glass wind chime.

Men are a different story altogether. They are the how and the howl. They are terrifying at first, in a thrilling way; and then later, after a few rough experiences, they become terrifying in a different way. Your interest in men blossoms once you begin to feel more at home in your body, even before you take the estradiol and the spironolactone, to flower the nectar of your estrogen and to extract the venom of your testosterone, and your cock metamorphosizes into a clit. That certainly accelerated your desires. But when you begin to see yourself through a mirror, as a woman, then you are able to at last stake claim to what you want. Even if it still makes you anxious in the moments leading up to being held. And then you can feel locked in place, at least for a little while.

That is the plan at least.

To have someone lock you in place.

Next is a series of trainwrecks that you willingly partake in. One part of your mind floats through the wreckage, and the next wreckage, and the next. You are always amazed and a bit skeptical when your transness seems to have no bearing on how they consider you, as they are too busy with their own obsessions to notice that you used to be a man. Your ability, or even willingness, to have high standards begins to fade, feel gauche. Fascination arises toward people who are ill-fitting and perhaps broken in a different way than you have been broken. And their idea of how to piece their lives back together is vastly different from yours—if they even want to. The knowledge of this doesn't compel you to stop throwing weighted dice. Throwing, throwing, throwing.

When you start to reach out to men, looking for more than mere fucking, and find that men still want you for the wrong reasons and only the wrong reasons, Aveline finds you. After a couple of dates she isn't sure what to make of you, but she continues anyway. Conversely, you are grateful to be touched. She touches you more forcefully. She keeps her secrets. But she wants you, and you want her, because you take her desire as a form of strength that you can rely on when you feel like you have none. You could inhabit the space of someone else's desire.

After a few months this desire of hers becomes hitting you. She has few interests besides nominally consensual violence and food. You agree to the violence. You agree to be hit, to be tied to her bedposts. What are you seeking to find here? The bruises she leaves are the color of plums. In being tied down, you long for escape.

When you leave her, at long last—by the skin of your teeth—you are miserable through the winter after. You try to decide how much attention you should pay to Aveline—not the real one, but the wraith of her that lived in the barrow of your empty heart. It's minus-twenty outside. January and February here are months of living on the moon—arid storms, bitter winds, long preparations to go to the grocery store. You have to act accordingly. Move slowly and deliberately. Your jacket has lost a button and it's half-useless and you can't afford a coat expensive enough to keep you warm. You stumble through. You have a few dates fall through. The silence and darkness of winter give you a space to try to work out what happened, but you don't see it as a gift.

Only when spring arrives—evolving into wet snow, sudden days in the forties that feel tropical—do you at last realize that you didn't want to be hit, that this submission wasn't who you were, but rather an idea that someone else had of you. Spring rivers are full of floes but the lakes remain steadfast. On some lakes there are full, thick sheets of ice until mid-April, and there are always a few trucks or snowmobiles that plunge through the cracks by men who want to push their luck or feel invincibly stubborn.

If this story is a romance, it's because a person you have not yet met—and, frankly, may never meet—has fallen in love with you. It could be like a stalker but it's not like that, not really. At the same time, this person doesn't exist yet. You are never entirely sure if this is a romance.

The last thing you want to do is choreograph a fake redemption story on your Facebook feed in order to garner sympathy for a problem you're going to solve anyway. Well, the sympathy from others would be sincere, heartfelt. But it would be unearned. Totally unearned. You don't want acquaintances even—to say nothing of your close friends—to expend encouragement under a false bill of goods, which would be this: treating your wounds not as an orchidial abyss but rather as a *platform*. It's another matter altogether, certainly, to confide in a friend or two. But that's not the issue here. You vow never to go fishing for sympathy. Never never never.

No, you want the encouragement to come *unbidden*.

In this light, you are no one's idea of a good time. Or a few people's but a small enough sample to be statistically insignificant. Even if you were to strike up a conversation with a man in the produce aisle, if he were to find out you were trans, the conversation would not last long, or go well, or maybe you would die. At some point, you lost heart in throwing the dice quite so fervently as you used to, when you reveled in the very possibility of a man kissing you, or wanting to kiss you.

Now, now—you have better things to do than waste your time. Now you signal your intentions and gender from a distance, like the hunters who wear fluorescent orange during deer season, so the men would not shoot each other. This meant that you were not a deer; the deer could not see the orange, and thus could not be startled by it. At any rate, you didn't want to be shot. You let them know who you were. This was crucial because you had a girl-dick. You didn't want to be gutted when a man discovered your girl-dick, or found any sort of opportunity, born of rage, to murder you or choke you out. So you let them pass by at a distance. And you didn't try to engage with the men at the grocery store or in line while getting coffee.

There always were a few exceptions. There always are. They were soft, tender boys with soft curls and graduate degrees. They seemed to understand you—to want you, through their own discernment of you.

And that was, in the end, the undoing. They knew about the other men, the ones who despised you. Instead, they considered themselves the deer who would nuzzle against your neck. But in return they wanted you to put down your defenses, not because they would protect you but because your fear of the other men made them uncomfortable. When you didn't acknowledge the fullness and splendor of the gentleness, they yelped at you and withdrew, which at times made you feel worse than

Anya Johanna DeNiro

the killers, who at the very least signaled their intentions clearly.

Also these men could not fuck you worth a dime.

Most times they never got to this stage. Instead they would forget you existed. They ended up saving their tenderness up, all up, and a year later you'd see them in the produce aisle, arm-in-arm with a willowy cis woman who used her parents' seed money to start a ceramics studio. One time you were going on a second date with one of these deer-boys, and you knocked on the door of his house to pick him up, and he didn't answer the door, even though you had texted him only twenty minutes before. Perplexed, you drove away from the dark house. An hour later he texted back and said that he had just gotten a tattoo and, for reasons mysterious, needed to lie down on the floor and not move in any way. He sent a bare-shirted picture of his new tattoo of a raven and you deleted every trace of him. Maybe, you reasoned afterward, this had nothing to do with you being trans—imagining his trembling hesitation, his faltering excuses and hour-long vow of monastic silence when you were standing on his door jamb— but you would never know. You would never know, or plumb these intentions, or the secret fears that well-meaning boys might have about putting their hands on your hips.

All the same, you still traipsed those winter woods. All the same. And every once in a while, as if the past has no meaning, and all that matters is the weak light of the sun hanging in the sky like a white coin, and the hunter who approaches you from behind—somehow he snuck up on you—and whistles, so as not to startle you.

He leans his rifle against a tree and holds up his hands, as if surrendering. And maybe he is. You put down your own gun and approach him. It looks like there is an emotion breaking over his face, though you can't tell which one it is. That turns out, in that moment, in the snow, to be enough for you, and you kneel in front of him and look up. And you put your hands on his cock through his Carhartts.

After he comes on your face, he doesn't look at you, and so you decide you don't want to look at him. Then the two of you collect yourselves, and your weapons, and go your separate ways.

They stare at you, they're always staring at you, in the ALDI, at the auto body shop, waiting for the nitro cold press in the Starbucks. *Just wait till they're through with you.*

"Insufficient funds."

You want to be fucked so badly.

You tell yourself that you're trying, but you keep failing at trying to try.

Just like the guys who are trying to want to fuck you. As it turns out you're a horrible judge of character, simply awful. How many potential partners have you passed on, and conversely, how many awful dates did you suffer through because of the certainty of your hunches? You keep thinking you're going to get better at it, but no. No!

Capture yourself over and over. Have to find the right cadence. Photos 1–5: light not right. 6: Readjust. Is that a beard shadow along the jawline? Ugh. Again. 7–10: Try without glasses.

Dried chrysanthemum blossoms fall onto your little car—when you turn on your windshield wiper as you start driving, they scatter behind you like pixels into the summer air. It's sweltering now. The seasons are drunkenly collapsing into the wrong beds. Summer's body is draped over winter's thigh. Spring spoons fall, who twitches in its sleep.

As you drive you think of one time in one of those last dishwashing summers—home from your MFA program, the last summer you stayed with your parents, actually—at the lone coffee shop in town. It was an open poetry reading, packed in the tiny space. Really the only game in town for the literary arts in a fifty-mile radius. The summer air outside was warm off the lake, gray and muggy. You brought some of your workshop poems and you were arrogant, so arrogant. The poems were well received. Eventually it came down to you and another guy for "audience choice of the night." He was a couple of years younger than you; you don't remember anything about his writing, except that you despised it. But more than that—he had an easy gait and confidence as a kind of scaffolding for his poems that you could only dream about possessing, which allowed him, in all likelihood, to win the final "read off" between the two of you. The winner was determined from applause volume in the room, and he was the clear winner. You shook his hand amicably while you seethed inside that your precocious, ultimately garden-variety Charles Simic pastiches didn't turn the tide of adulation your way. Were his poems garden-variety Bukowski pastiches, you wonder. Yes, in all likelihood. Indeed! He also didn't seem to recognize that you were *professionally* and *objectively* (as you grandly considered it at the time) better than him at writing poems. You realized that he saw your poems solely through the realm of the city where he likely lived, and that you were on the verge of leaving for good, that he had no inner Rosetta Stone for reading even a pretty mainstream poet like Charles Simic. Your parents' city, the city you were trying to hard to escape with your airs and your shaming. He had no way of knowing. The city, you thought, was in a bubble of its own making. Many times you have been surprised that airplanes from other cities actually land there, that there *are* connections to other cities, that connective tissue exists. Your own connections frayed.

The men who are quick to say *we are just borrowing our bodies, I'm incredibly open-minded* will not touch you. In fact they're repulsed by the very thought of touching you. As if you can impregnate a man with sexual discomfort. When the man tells you on a dating site *Sorry I don't swing that way* or *I'm not interested in men,* even when you have no real intention of contacting him, he is really trying to tell you *You are alone.* He had to let you know that you were alone. He felt compelled to cut you off the pass, just to make sure there wasn't any misunderstanding about his intentions or sexuality. This is not unusual. This is not a special case. This romance is not unique. Its storybooks are printed and bound with the scrim of chat rooms, cam sites, swipes right, the likes, the stars filled in—unfilled again.

But see here, you. The funny thing—and if you really stop to think about it, it's really fucking funny—is that you're not alone.

He's alone.

You know he's alone because you used to be alone just like him. Or just enough like him to know. And although it's not worth terribly too much of your time, it's worth considering for a moment that he has no real way to know what he wants, as he sits in his Acura in the parking lot of a Texas Roadhouse, texting bile, the emptiness leaking out like barrels in a Superfund site.

One weekend you have time on your hands so you try to disassemble the camera obscura the best you can. You still feel disassembled yourself. You're not very skilled at being alone.

"Dad?" you say.

He stares at the camera obscura, pursing his lips.

"Why do you want to take this apart again, now? I have to say, it's a neat little contraption. Very inventive."

You consider telling him more about how you received the plans for it, but decide against it. "I don't

OKPsyche

want to always look through it. It's painful to have sitting here. But at the same time, maybe there's something in the parts that I can use. I'm tired."

He sits down on your futon. "Isn't everybody." He sighs. "Well, it would be quite a job, but I could. But why don't you put the coin inside?"

You're a bit surprised that your dad is actually being helpful. But you roll with it. Maybe the dead can grow too. Maybe the dead can change. "Sorry, what now?"

He points to the side of the camera obscura, where there's a slot and it says, in faded block type, "INSERT COIN."

Maybe your father had conjured it.

"Thanks, Dad. You mean it."

"Well." He rubs his head. "It's the least I could do."

You pause. "Do you want some coffee or anything?"

But he is no longer there.

You put the three-sided coin in and wait inside the obscura. Nothing happens for a good long while, but then you feel the wood and metal around you getting warmer, and then you find yourself in a pile of wet leaves, in the middle of a forest, waiting for the spirit to come.

It's okay to be alone and scared. You try to breathe naturally. You wait in the middle of the leaves and you start to get angry at your loneliness. You're angry because you have no fucking idea what you're supposed to be waiting for. You're buried in a pile of leaves hiding, gestating, *transitioning*. This estrogen rewiring you, this testosterone evicted. You hear a lot of other voices in the woods. You hear gentle voices, in groups of three or four who love each other and care for each other and feed each other food that they have grown. They have done the work to care for each other, you imagine. They are empathic and open with their fears and hopes and share lovers with ease and good communication and—

"Hey," a voice says. Someone is brushing leaves off your shoulders. You stand up. Look around in a daze. Twilight already. The voices are not in the woods anymore, or at least you don't hear them. Standing in front of you is a very tall person, the one you saw in the bar you hated. They're no longer wearing a floppy hat or a shawl. Instead they wear the shimmering violet gown of a queen.

"Hi," you say, standing up.

"I got your message," they say. "Come on."

You pick off leaves, and you walk together for a while. You look over at the couples having a picnic in a grove. They all look incredibly happy and calm as they share unfamiliar, glistening red and pink fruits. One of the women in one of the couples is Kierney, clapping while telling a joke. She doesn't seem to notice you.

"Don't worry about them," they say quietly. "That's not why you're here."

You don't want to ask too many questions as to why you're here. You pass a young woman hunched over in an armchair along the trail, and you can't tell if she's turning a lily into a knife or the other way around.

They take you to a beech tree grove, towering over you, where there's an old tattered sofa. You both sit. They ask you what you need.

"A boyfriend," you say, not hesitating because you're afraid the words will stick in your mouth otherwise.

They stare at you.

"Or a girlfriend," you say quickly. "Just . . . someone."

"Oh, for fuck's sake," they snort. "You little bitch. You little bitch."

"Excuse me?" you say.

"The planet is dying!" they shout, standing up from the couch, the beech leaves vibrating around them. "In no short amount of time, the firmament of the earth will groan and break with the carcasses of all the species we have slain, trans women are locked in cages at the border and murdered on the streets, trans kids are shoved back in the closet on an industrial scale, and you're worried about a *boyfriend?*"

"Well—" you start to say.

"You think this heteronormative box-checking will save you?" they say, pacing the couch. "That candlelit dinners in normal restaurants with good lighting will save you? That going to meet a man's parents on Thanksgiving will save you? That if anyone on the street laughs at you this boyfriend is going to beat the shit out them?"

"I don't want to be alone!" you shout at them. "I am . . . fucking alone." You look around the grove. All of the emptiness rushes upward. "Then maybe if I feel less alone, I can help others? I don't know."

They sigh and touch your cheek. "You know, you're never alone. You know that, right?"

"Yes," you say. "I believe it, but also I lack certainty. My brain tricks me."

"It tricks us all," they say. They roll their tongue around in their mouth. "Tell you what. We can get you the boyfriend. *But* you'd have to assemble him yourself."

You're suddenly timid from your impetuous demands for comfort. "I don't really need—"

"Just fucking take it," they say. "We'll mail you the rest of the materials and the instructions."

You nod.

"It's okay," they say. "Do what you can, when you can. But you don't have to feel perfect inside to do it. Joan of Arc never had a self-care regimen."

She exhales, like blowing out the seeds of a dandelion. You wake up rigid on your bed. You hurry outside to taste the night air, taste the honking of distant horns, the choppers hovering over the city which might be federal or commercial or personal. Even through the night hazes you can see the stars. The stars float by like cottonwood, like the Pleiades at last unleashed.

That is the easy part. Now the easy part is over and the hard part is coming. This is a slight intermission. There won't be verses, there won't be poetry, there will only be burning forests, and a rain of ash.

People are allowed to be happy.

Once you were a child at the deer camp, which your grandparents owned, in the middle of an old-growth national forest. You'd find abandoned shacks at the end of logging trails. Campfire bacon and antlers mounted on the walls. The whole family would cut down dead trees with chainsaws, split the logs. The kids would haul the wood into the truck. Driving up the mountain in the back of the pickup. The cold air that came at midnight. Finding shotgun shells in clearings. Coming across black bear tracks. Going "spotting" for deer late at night, all the kids loaded in the back of the pickup truck to shine spotlights into fields. Sometimes you would see a dozen at a time. Once you saw an albino doe, majestic in an ambling herd.

In the summers you would spend a week at a time up at the camp. Your dad would come up occasionally on weekends. But he always felt like an outsider to your mother's family.

In winter, the camp became a place for the men of the family to enter the woods and kill deer and drink and return. They'd come back with the deer carcass in the back of the truck to be processed. The only part that wasn't frozen stiff was the eye, and you would take turns touching the eye.

Sometimes you wonder whether you will, at a point in the future, learn how to shoot a rifle again. Whether this will become important again, whether for food or to keep the blood inside your body. Not as a boy who never learned to hunt, but as a woman.

A few days later you receive a large UPS package. There is no return address. The package is heavy and dense, about the size of a sheepdog lying down. After you drag it into your apartment, you cut it open and it begins to fill in more space. Another layer of thick plastic wrapping. Cutting this away you are filled with unease and embarrassment as you realize what this is, and who sent it. It's a man, about forty years of age, perfectly folded in on himself at the waist. His body is a bit flattened, like an inner tube that still needs air, the pneumatic transfer of someone's breath. You stare at his face and touch his cheek. The skin is warm.

He's pretty. There's no doubt about that.

Taped to his chest is a set of instructions in about six languages, in a small grainy script. There are diagrams that depict beams of light refracted by a heart. You look on the back, then the front again, and the instructions change. You do this over and over and realize that the instructions in English are about fifteen pages long. You sigh. Why is he warm? What does he need? How do you attend to him when he is not awake, but still in your care?

You push the box to your bedroom and slide him under the bed. Your boyfriend will have to wait another day.

A few days later you're convinced you're going to at last die at the hands of a man. A man convinces you of this when he follows you in the park and threatens to kill you and everyone like you. You're walking through a massive park next to the college—usually it's full of students, but it's spring break, it's clear empty, and the man walking behind you is wearing a black hoodie, baseball hat, he's white, and he starts talking about you. He tells you

OKPsyche

how much he fucking despises you and how he wants to
kill you and every other trans person in the world, and
for about half a minute as you walk you're sure that you
are going to bleed to death or be strangled or shot at
his hands, right at that moment. A few of the passersby
around him look at him, look at you, but they don't stop
walking. You're afraid to turn around. Instead you walk
to the wall of the student union building and pretend to
look at your phone.

He keeps walking, muttering. He doesn't turn toward
you. He is an arrow that has been loosened and doesn't
veer from its path, and you are lucky enough to get out
of the way.

You wonder if being arm-in-arm with a man or a
woman would have inoculated you from these verbal
assaults. Whether that's what it comes down to. When
you dated Aveline, she had said more than once that
she would fuck up anyone who tried to hurt you, and
you absolutely believed she was capable of it. That in
itself was thrilling and comforting, for a while. Until she
turned on you.

From your trans support group, and online, you know
that countless trans women have been ridiculed by the
police when asking for help, even after being assaulted.
Or their bodies are found in dumpsters later, or shot in
the face and left in the street, or burned into char. They
get choked and then laughed at by the police, they think
that the trans women have it coming for them because
they believe very strongly that trans women are nothing but a trick to be played on men, and when the trick
is done men can do anything they want to them—choke
and murder, and mutilate.

These women are almost never white, and you know this, you know that if you get ridiculed they might get punched in the face, and if you ever got punched in the face they might get shot. It's not the same. It's never the same. You walk toward the flower beds at the center of the park after you're sure he's passed far away, and you stare hard at the tulips of late March, golden apelboorn and ballade, huis ten bosch and verona.Tired of shaving the face, the cuts, the endless cuts, and the burns, you subject yourself to sitting on a massage table while lasers burn off the hairs on your face. But only the darker ones. The whiter ones stay. Burn, burn them off. The only way is through, and a hundred bees stinging a single point on your face at once. Burn.

"Sorry!" the aesthetician says. She does sound apologetic, in a practiced way. Ten years ago the clinic would have never catered to trans women. They would have laughed you out of the lobby if you asked for their services. You suppose that's progress, for white trans women at least—that you can masquerade as a soccer mom from Edina for twenty minutes in a quasi-clinical capacity while you take your licks to make yourself beautiful. Or at least make yourself easier to bear in the morning when you see the shadows along your jawline, your lip. The pain, for a woman, is supposed to be salutary, and you are thrilled that you are able to participate, with your own means, your own debt.

Don't you fucking stop with the burning.

As you keep the hot young man under the bed, you start dating Hannah. You imagine yourself arcing toward your future but you're not sure which one. But in the end, it's certainly not with a man—at least, not one you've ever found in the flesh, imbued with a soul.

You know it's probably not going to last very long with Hannah but it's mitigated by the fact that she doesn't hate herself.

Hannah also has a fierceness and directness that surpasses Aveline's, but she loves herself, and you find this a refreshing change of pace. It doesn't require mentioning that she accepts you completely as you are. If you stopped to think about it, this would be shocking to you a mere year ago. During a long marriage to a dull man, and a child, she had decided to date other interesting men and women at the same time, and found a community that suited her. She laughs easily. She builds things: dresses with pockets, jigsaw puzzles, music boxes, hidden safes inside books.

Every once in a while you would squint and imagine yourself as a part of her circle more permanently. She lives alone by choice, even though she has a partner and a girlfriend, and an archipelago of others who they date, or once dated. Once she shows you a flowchart of how everyone in her polycule was connected to each other, and it was like a star chart from the Age of Exploration.

"Are you *sure* you have the bandwidth for this?" you tell her on your first coffee date.

She lowers her gaze at you. "I wouldn't be here if I didn't."

But she doesn't. You really don't blame her for only realizing this after the fact, but she doesn't. When she breaks things off with you a couple of months later, you remind her of what she said.

"I know!" she says. "I know. I'm so, so sorry. I didn't know until I did it."

If you could have just made your way into this group, you reasoned, then you could have all the cis people you wanted in your life and more, to fuck and hold and cook for and care for. And then you could find a boyfriend, who had probably dated Hannah before, while still having a girlfriend, and everything would have worked out. You would have been one more star in the star chart, that other people would navigate by.

But you realized much later that Hannah not only broke up with you because of the fact that your mutual schedules would not align. For most of your life you were worried about being left out. The bouncers at bars would always look at you askance when you were pretending inelegantly to be a man. They would concoct arbitrary excuses to keep you out. The panic would be on your face even before you reached the door, and the prophecy would fulfill itself, and you would head home ashamed when your friends went inside with apologetic faces. And yet at other times you were completely invisible, for example when you wanted to gain anyone's attention. Even at a checkout counter. The contradiction in these two social presences drove you to such despair that you reckoned—if you could imagine yourself in the right way, then others would be forced to do the same. Of course, for a painfully long time you had no idea that this involved shaving your body hair, wearing wigs, and taking pills in order to melt down the man you were, and in the cooled, sublimated substance, fashion yourself into an actual form in which you didn't despise yourself.

The answer was right there, for the longest time.

Anyway, Hannah and her polycule brought this out in you, through no fault of her own. She had her own agency that was purposeful and gave no quarter to bullshit. But perhaps she knew that you knew that you'd never fit in, that fitting in would have been a form of slow unhappiness, that you had to earn your own circle of caring people, your own star chart that would lead you to voyage somewhere else, somewhere else you needed to be more than anything.

In order to bodily deny the fact that they were trans—to masquerade *harder* as being normal and cis, nothing to see here—some of the trans women you knew joined the Marines, bought a motorcycle, or took up bodybuilding or bodybuilding forums. You, on the other hand, started reading theology in earnest.

Your path was by far the most ridiculous.

But it never works. The dam always breaks.

After trying to make God the Father come back to you, it becomes clearer and clearer that King God has left you. There is no place for God in you. God used to fill in all the cracks of you, God made a fool out of you and a believer out of you, but you are no longer small and hollow and easy to fill up. When you began to transition you realized that you could not have God concurrently with being transgender, because you wanted all the things that God didn't want for you, for example men cumming down your throat, men biting down on your nipples and clamping their teeth there.

You just figured God did not want any of these things for you, that it was slightly embarrassed by you. It seemed like a reasonable assumption. You try to imagine a God that *does* want these things for you, and you just can't. You do not carry shame like you used to. Any shame you express becomes a form of play. Or at least attempted play.

You have to think God has left people for worse reasons.

All the same, if God did want these things for you, you would not trust it. Maybe you have these old idolatries. These golden calves. But you've been calmer, more centered since God has left you. More reasonable and less afraid. With God there is always fear. Not fear of fucking up but the fear of being *really good* at piety. Once you succeed you are *in*. You are inside God and you have to completely reconfigure your life—legally, endocrinologically—to exorcise God.

Any God of affirmation is not your God, because God is not Lord, God is not King of Kings, but something else. Something awful and stupid.

When you were just starting to transition you made a last-ditch effort to keep God in your heart before it would leave you forever, through Christian "death of God" theology. Radical theology, largely for men, as you understood it. You thought that you could make that work as you were finding your way to womanhood. That thinking about God in this fashion would make leaving everything you knew behind somehow less terrifying. And this way you would wait for God to eliminate itself inside your heart. An odd way to hold God close, unless you remember that God would have been able to keep the corpse and do anything He wanted with it.

You would pray the Lord's Prayer every night right before you fell asleep well into your forties. You would try to find the meaning there in that consistency and miserable panic right before shutting your eyes, before a long night of restless sleep. You didn't believe in the resurrection of the flesh or Jesus but you still believed in God.

Now you can't remember the words anymore. You used to pray to be struck down. Now you take walks.

The night is inside the music, and the music is inside of you. It fireflows. Can they see the faintest traces of scruffy face in this light, the shadow that you've smeared with concealer? Don't know. Probably.

You're expected to play ball. Get along. Going into the nightclub. It's been many months since your breakup. You're wearing the sub collar you bought for ten dollars on eBay. It has a snap instead of a buckle. It's a hell of a prop, considering who you used to be. It has a metal heart with two tinkling chains on either side. You wear a red leather jacket you got for fifteen dollars at a thrift store. Your driver's license picture matches your face for the most part. Same jacket at least. It's late spring. Warmth has finally started to sublimate the air. You are meeting friends. They care about you. Other people may or may not appear in your orbit. They matter to you too. After you started transitioning you began to realize how little everyone else was concerned about your gender. You don't have anything to worry about from people who actually care about you. You will die. You cut down on your mistakes. Friends can begin to see you for who you are, and still you don't have anything to worry about.

"You haven't changed much at all," your friend says. Since you asked her whether you had changed. Why does this sting? She sees it as a positive, and you try to take it as such. The light inside the club is milky and dark. You are in the middle of a conversation involving your work. You think of your father and frailness at the end. How he couldn't hold a Styrofoam cup at the end. You admit to yourself you weren't around at all. You admit to yourself you stayed away.

You dance. You shake inside your hips and then out.

A man dances with you, close to you, and he puts your hand down his pants. And you let him, you let him, you want to not let him, and even in your drunkenness there is shame, but you have held a cock in your hand so rarely that you want to hold it, until your friend pulls the two of you away and you never wish to see the man again.

You only remember this happens the next afternoon while—

"I told him to get the fuck off you," your friend Kite says.

"Jesus," your other friend says. "Fuck guys."

And it becomes apparent to you that you do have friends now. Though you feel sick and ashamed of yourself for being only vaguely repulsed by the man on the dance floor. For far too long you have preemptively bared your throat to those who have deserved no such gesture from you.

*

Kite is a true friend, a true person. She's no Kierney. You only met her that night, in fact. It's in quotidian details that you're quite sure that she's real—she swore at men, she straightened the collar of your red jacket, she bought you a drink.

"You're real, right?" you say, as you're both leaning forward at the bar.

"Sure am," she shouts over the music. "Are you?"

You laugh, and when she hands you a vodka tonic you tap plastic cups with her.

She tells you that she's trans. You weren't sure. You nod and tell her that you are too. You find this self-evident, but she says: "I was pretty sure, but not totally. But—what does it matter, right?"

"For sure," you say. What does it matter. For a fleeting moment or two, it escapes you.

You look around at the club. You always thought that you wanted these spaces at one a.m. But the lights do go up again. The hallways painted black are swept then mopped. Your blink, over and over, and stumble out. All the goth kids from Edina stumble out

In the jumble outside waiting for cars, you and Kite exchange numbers on your phones.

"This is great," she says. "We should totally hang out!"

"For sure," you say, giving her a quick hug, and you fully expect to never hear from her again. But you do.

The hormones accomplish their slow work of erasures and accretions. The redevelopment, the palimpsest overtaking the original lettering. And your anger, clear at last, and malleable. The boy box stays underneath your bed, like a man in a coffin, expectant. The burial of who you used to be is slow work, but also clarifying.

You want to reach the point where your deadname no longer haunts you.

History is nothing more than the venom of a dying bee, piercing the flesh of time. Everything that could have known about nearly all women like you has been lost. It was lost the moment they died of old age, or smallpox, or the cleft of an axe, as no records were kept of them. Nearly everything that could have happened throughout most of time has not been written down. Women were to act as exemplars for moral behavior, and also property for a man to gaze upon occasionally, and in other cases touch.

And yet, despite this legal demarcation disguised as a sacred writ, wanting to become a woman could only be described as an aberration at best. Why would a man want to become property? What man would want to become less than a dog?

Things are not so cut and dried, though. At one time there was a continuum between substances that made their transmutation easier. Breast milk was considered purified menstrual blood. And moreover, if men were considered hot and dry according to the humors, then transition could be accomplished by cooling the blood, the phlegm, the yellow bile, and the black bile. And the desire to undertake this would itself be a sign of womanhood. Learned men in Pisa and Cordoba indicated that male and female sex organs were also on the same continuum—the vagina was the penis turned inside out. And that women, when having sex, also released seed.

And you know it's not consistent. It's never consistent. All you ask for is the space to develop a private mythology, whether in the woods or no, one where you can consume what you need to survive.

III.

Once, over the course of several years before you came out to yourself, you wrote the first third of a novel in which a man and woman who were in love switched genders. Obviously, looking back, the sightlines were painfully obvious, a near-photographic transmission of your desires and losses into the actual, legible world in the only way that you knew how at the time: writing incomplete novels.

The novel was called *World Fantasy*.

The man and woman met at a small gallery in Minneapolis that somehow managed to pull off an exhibition of still lives from Haarlem in the late seventeenth century. A suicide bomber blew up the paintings, and severely injured Mark and Henrietta, who before that had been strangers. He was a security guard at the gallery, and she worked at a consultancy that advised a popular MMORPG. They fell in love. They started sticking to each other, literally and viscerally.

But you were too afraid to go on.

God, you were too afraid!

*

Anya Johanna DeNiro

In the scheme of things, though you don't write anymore, you imagine that men give themselves permission
to write anything they want. Maybe you used to be the
same way, but you almost forced yourself to forget how.
They could write novels that consist of a single sentence;
they could insert themselves into the story in an awkward way, in order to make the reader more aware that
they are fretting and equivocating that they are in the
story, and including other pieces of their fiction in the
story and fucking women who somehow appreciate their
company; they can embody an easy, cheerful numbness;
they can transform the writing of metafiction into a two-
bedroom apartment that's a pleasant ten-minute walk
from the campus of a land-grant university. And if those
things do not happen in actuality, the dream of them
happening tantalized you and haunted you, for a while.
You thought you could attain them, and it would stop
the gyre inside of you that threatened to suck everything
inside.

But you had passed the threshold, and realized that
you had never belonged. Or rather, when you at last
gave yourself permission to understand that you would
never belong, the need to write in order to demonstrate
to yourself that you were "surviving," that you weren't in
fact ignoring every sign that you were a woman, could be
cast away. And you stopped writing. One day, it simply
didn't occur to you to write anymore, the end.

The aftermath was much easier, though the hard work
became of a much different sort. It was the hard work of
allowing yourself to be maudlin and ridiculous, to sow
the hard ground of your past with a viaduct of tears. It
was the hard work of being embarrassing. This was the

pact with your body, your skin and hips accelerating into a more agreeable form. Your body wasn't a myth.

And you knew that if you exited your bedroom with imperfectly applied eyeliner and blush, in a red Goodwill dress that didn't quite fit you right, into the street, the very air around you turned into a query.

People felt they deserved to reckon with you.

Into the street—who knows who might have been there? Certainly people who didn't know the panoply of your journey. They smirk or snicker as you pass. One man shouting behind you: *You're not fooling anybody!*

But still, you took your hormones every day, and the testosterone died on the vine, and the estrogen came into blossom, filling the once-poisoned vessel of your body. You knew that this itself was a gift, an accident, even with all of your work—plenty of other women like you could not afford this or would have this balm denied to them by doctors and pastors and pharmacists. They could be anywhere, but they often huddled together in pews.

That is, on some days, who you imagine your boy in the box to fight against, or at least repel.

Maybe that was all you ever wanted.

You crumple every word you've ever written as a man—denser, denser—into the size of a gumball. You put it on your bookshelf, behind the books of continental philosophy, hidden away so your cat will not play with it. She will play with anything.

*

These changes are not baroque shocks—the changes are instead the warm thrums of a heavy wool blanket pulled up tight against the unrelenting cold.

Psyche, tired of being painted, tired of other people's allegories, goes on the run from Cupid and the other minor gods, takes a horse over the Alps from Milan. She is running for her life—for her own conception of her life—away from the capricious gods and goddesses, to find a place where she can settle into her own thoughts.

But what of love, Cupid mewls. *What of my desires, don't you care about my desires—*

Don't you run away from my son, Aphrodite shouts. *Look at me. Look at me. Show some respect.*

Psyche, crossing the Alps, ends up in Eindhoven in southern Holland, asleep by a fire on the lower floor of a tavern, where Van Gogh used to live, where he painted the potato farmers, the poorest of the poor.

You are allowed to like things you once liked. It's hard but permissible.

One day, your ex-wife calls.

"Hello, _____? Is that you?"

"Hi, Mary," you say. "It's me."

"I . . . didn't recognize your voice."

"I guess it's changed?" you say, not sure of what to say. You haven't been working on your voice since you spoke to her last a few weeks ago. You didn't have a coach. You didn't go Japan for tens of thousands of dollars' worth of surgery on your vocal cords, out of pocket—

"Okay," she says. You can hear her taking a deep breath. Movement behind her on the line. Masking tape getting stretched out. Is that your son with a school project? "So, I'll get right to the point. Aaron and I are going to be visiting Minnesota for a week. I'm going to be staying with my parents."

"I . . ." You trail off, and try to begin again, but you can't. Eventually you say: "Jerry. What about Jerry?" Her boyfriend. The carpenter.

"He . . ." You can hear her turn her head away from the phone and cough. "Yeah. It just didn't work out between us."

"I'm sorry," you say. And in a moment of intense surprise for yourself, you really are.

"It's okay," she says. "Things happen for a reason. Don't they?"

"I suppose they do," you say.

And you remind yourself you *did* love before. You loved your wife. You were not bereft of love. But after you came out, at first to yourself, and then in a widening circle, you began an inexorable process of becoming a person your wife didn't know. More than that—when you revealed your past self, the one she loved, to her, you revealed yourself being as much of a compromised persona as a human being consumed by shame.

You made your shame legible. That became the project at first—not to transition to womanhood right away (you had no idea how to go about it at the riptide speeds other trans friends of yours took on) but to let yourself find a place for the shame. And to read it out loud and acknowledge it and allow yourself to be someone else— not devoid of the secret history but unchained from it.

"Yeah. They do," you say. "So . . ."

"So what happens with us?" she says, completing your sentence, which she always had a knack for, sometimes for good, sometimes for ill. "As parents," she quickly adds, though that of course is obvious.

"I want to be part of Aaron's life more," you say, imagining yourself giving a decree on the temple steps for a goddess's festival, clear and unabashed. Imploring action. A few years ago you would not have been able to be this direct.

"I know," she says. "So, look, while we're in the city, why don't you and Aaron . . . spend an afternoon together? Maybe an overnight? Just some . . . parent-son bonding time."

You realize that she still can't call you a mother.

"Sure," you say. "I'd love that."

The pleasures of your mind become obscured when you're 50K in medical debt. And this debt has nothing to do with transition, but rather your son's health problems right after he was born. The problems with breath. The fairy-sized CPAP mask he had to wear in the NICU.

On the night he was born you followed in your subcompact Honda in the wake of his hospital transfer in the ambulance, then traversing the snowfall and the empty courtyards of the children's hospital after you parked.

On the night he was born you read *Goodnight Moon* to him in a shaky voice, and soon after fell asleep in a chair.

On the night he was born you touched his hand with your thumb, positioning your arm inside the incubator. His hand was the size of a penny.

On account of that debt, and the hold it continues to have on your life, you feel awkward in upper-middle-class social circumstances that you sometimes orbit around, many times by accident. You are at a reception the day after you talk to your ex. You are receiving and being received. A reading given by an acclaimed writer at a ramblingly large house in south Minneapolis. The writer is a friend of the person who lives here. His actual reading is at a bookstore in the city the next day, ticketed and sold out.

No one knows who you are, in fact you are only vaguely aware of the form and style of the writer himself, but everyone is kind.

You're terrified of being recognized from your old life, but you see no one that you used to know.

You got the invite from a friend of a friend of Hannah's, you're surprised when she presents you with it—but you're not sure why you accepted it once you get there. Maybe you imagine that being social will be fruitful.

Instead, it's all easy, dire civility, and you're ignored. Swarms surround the writer, and the host who is also a writer, everyone is a writer, except you perhaps. You were far more interested in the Edwardian home than the writers, the writers' conversations. The photos on the wall of vacations, the oil paintings on the walls from their painter friends, or woodcuts from woodcut friends.

You feel like a feral she-wolf who has wandered into a house full of anchor partners. You are not a significant other—you are just an other.

Your house was not altogether clean, nor put together. You were never sure why. When you were married and raising Aaron together, you'd look at houses like this— *able to receive guests*—and feel embarrassed that you could never quite get your shit together, architecturally and otherwise.

Declaring that you had class embarrassment and debt embarrassment and house embarrassment with this group of mostly white homeowners in their forties would have been itself embarrassing. People were not supposed to talk about such things in the Midwest. Instead it became sublimated and dispersed, like traces of antidepressants and estrogen in the American water supply.

Living alone has given you the wherewithal to clean your apartment regularly.

It is much smaller. There is no useless, brambled lawn, no mulberry trees run wild. No empty storage closets with books and boxes stacked in front of it.

But maybe transitioning has had something to with it as well—not in terms of any feminine role of housekeeping you've taken the mantle of, god forbid. But rather that, when living as a man, the squalor around you matched your own inner state, and you were willing to tolerate it.

A man and a woman on a purple davenport compare agents and advances. Another circle: vacations in Mexico, comparison of, by region. And *what school do your kids go to* being the question of choice to talk about whiteness and social class without actually mentioning it directly.

For so long you craved the trappings of Minneapolis that they had. You took the surfaces that other people presented to the world as writ.

You give a stiff smile as you wade around people as they block the door to the kitchen with the center island and granite countertops full of charcuterie and Merlot bottles. Do these things matter? As you fumble in the refrigerator for a beer, an older man, holding court in the corner, decides to strike up a conversation with you. You are wearing a dark yellow dress with a black scarf. He asks your name.

"_____! That's such an unusual name! What does it mean? Where does it come from?"

What does any name mean? You look for a bottle opener on the counter as you answer. "It's Slavic. My mom's side of the family is Slavic." And then, offering to this man more than he deserves: "I chose the name myself, though."

Immediately, you see his curiosity piqued, and your heart falls. "Oh! What was your name before? You have to tell me!"

"No," you say, looking away.

He doesn't know. He really doesn't know. Or otherwise he is playing a cruel long con. You don't think it's the latter—these pleasant writerly circumstances do not lend themselves to bullying trans people, at least that outwardly. And he has probably not done the equation in his head as to why a woman would change her first name. For him—professor at a writing program, local university, published occasionally by a local university press, you imagine—he doesn't have the good sense to figure it out.

He looks at you as if you're ridiculous, capricious. You walk away into the living room, shaking. A small part of you, a voice that you're a bit ashamed of, is secretly happy that he didn't realize that you are trans. That you passed. You don't try to judge this pleasure—five years ago, you would have treasured it, even if it was from an awful, clueless man.

When you came out as trans your acquaintances were kind to you. They'd send supportive Facebook messages. You'd come home from work—*honey, I'm home*—and spy the mail stacked high on the ledge near the front door, and Aaron's LEGOs strewn on the living room floor like a diviner's sacred knucklebones, and dishes piled high in the sink, and fruit flies blasting out of the drain. You would dream all the time about sagging houses with floorboards that would break open revealing an unknown floor below, mold on the frames on the wall that had no paintings in them. You would dream of wandering through mostly abandoned shopping malls, looking for that one store to buy a lacquered fan.

You were lazy, there was no doubt about that. But the two of you could never quite get your act together.

You were the moon, and she was the sun.

And the stars were stigmata.

Trying to trace the dotted lines between stars that turned on and off. Trans women have their own

constellations. Under the light of those stars, you see
your lost girlhood.

The rest of the late afternoon and early evening at the
reception is a blur. You stagger to your car and drive
home. It's late spring, a confused season here. One
day it can snow, and another it can be shorts weather.
With more skin showing, when you're not bundled in a
heavy jacket and wool scarf, there is more of a chance to
be seen. Being trans lets everyone else know, if you're
clocked, to enact a surveillance protocol. To be wary.
Having suspicions aroused is one of the only ways they
have to get off. It's for protecting the community: Little
League baseball games, gun shows at the community
center, and the Cornflower Festival in mid-May. In
the Catholic grade school of your youth, it was Mary's
month, when she was crowned queen of heaven. There
would be a procession in the church with the statue of
Mary held aloft by the priest, the older schoolchildren
dressed in white. The veiled queen would be placed on
the altar. That night you would pray the rosary in your
bedroom of your own accord: the Joyful Mysteries,
the Sorrowful Mysteries, the Glorious Mysteries. You
realized much later that you grew up less in a Catholic Church than a Marian cult. Jesus the son was sec-
ondary to Mary the mother. You offered yourself to her,
over and over. During other times that month, a family
could sign out and take home in the evening, to pray the
rosary to. Yes, yes, it was for Mary's intercession to God,
not praying to Mary, yes, yes. The priest and Franciscan
nuns that taught you that, but almost with a wink. No,

no, we do not worship the mother of God, only a fool or a Baptist would think that. Mary was the comforter.

You go home and cut the tender echelons of an onion, scatter the chop on a hot pan. The simple work keeps your heart from turning invisible.

No uterus, no opinion, you read.

Before things were written down, people would fashion pottery—not for holding water or grain but to break into tiny pieces for their fields. Along with charcoal, the potsherds would replenish the land over time. And your own body does not hold the shape that it used to. The shape of how you held it in your mind and memory as a child when you were still growing, a puberty of terror. Your self would instead have to gain its use not out of the ability to contain other substances but to break and keep breaking and lay down the veil of shards that would allow something else to grow.

When you go deeper into malice, it scares you. This is not why you transitioned. You want to leave the malice behind.

You're careful not to display too awful or plain of a face, even when you're extremely upset. A way to be absolutely clear and inscrutable.

Your margins are thin. You have no money, nor boundless reserves of love and care, to cushion any falling-apart. When you do an in-store pickup at a place like Best Buy, where changing the name on your account seemed more trouble than it was worth—the person with your HDMI cables or DVD box set of *Berserk* or whatever would squint at you, and say, *picking up for* deadname *then?* And you'd say, without missing a beat, *yes, I'm his wife.* This both enthralled you and made you slightly ill, but for a couple seconds you allowed yourself to become betrothed. It was an easy lie to slip into, that you were married to yourself.

Your son was terrified of the future when you first transitioned. The future was almost too painful to think about. The words he said to you in terror—which were transmuted into anger—were curses. *You're a boy, you're a boy,* in sing-song. The worst curse that you could imagine. You wanted to be a normal mother, but it was not meant to be. Once you made toast for him and tried to make a smiley face in the peanut butter, but the face was more dazed than cheerful, and you thought to yourself: how could you fuck up something so normal, so motherly? When he got angry at you he would say: *I'm going to tell everyone in my class that you're really a boy.* For him that was the curse of curses. All of the pained words from his lips render you unable to forget them. *Thanks, "Dad." All you do is wear wigs.*

Then they left.

*

You had been afraid for a long time of them taking away everything you had tried so carefully to build up. All the edifices.

And then it had happened.

And yet, you lived.

For a long time you didn't even allow yourself the possibility of being a mother, of whatever sort. For a long time, motherhood became a bit more than you could hope for, as if you were flying to close to the sun or biting off more than you could chew by simply declaring motherhood, existing as a woman with a child of your own.

Your mother never wished you a happy Mother's Day, and when Aaron was away from you, you ended up dreading the day.

If you were not a father anymore—clearly—you dwelled in a space that was neither mother nor father, a kind of un-mother, and anti-father. It did not help that your son was so far away, so cut off from your everyday life.

You were afraid that passersby, repairmen, grocery cashiers, museum attendants, and others would cast judgment upon you with the deviltry of their own experiences. You shouldn't have let them affect you, to occupy a single tract of your imagination, but they did.

After a few years, you gained the ability to not give a fuck about what strangers thought about you and your appearance in the world. All the same, it took you a little time to catch up to your desire for motherhood, your capacity to hold it close to your heart like a lavalier.

Two weeks. They are coming in two weeks. You go to IKEA alone to refurbish your apartment, just in case the sleepover happens. You watch the straight couples that have just moved in together compare bookshelves. No imaginary trans women—or boyfriends—help you load the bed into the Prius. But still you hope that this won't be the only visit. Especially not now. You wander through the tableaus of ordinary, straightened life.

You still have no desire to put your boyfriend together. You find it comforting to have him present and readily available, in his own dormant way.

Maybe after the visit you'll give him the assembly that he requires.

You invite your new friend Kite over for tea. You haven't had people "over" for ages. The first thing you do, after giving her a beer, is show her the life-size doll in the suitcase. She doesn't say anything. Fragments of IKEA furniture are in half-formations all around you, like dinosaur skeletons in the middle of assemblage at the natural history museum.

"I'm sorry," you say, after a minute of silence between the two of you. You're both sitting on the floor, the suitcase between your bodies. "I'm so sorry."

"What the hell," she whispers.

"I'm sorry to put you through this."

"No, it's just—" She pauses. She brushes a hand over his dead cheek. "He's cute."

You snort. "Oh my God. Ah. Ah." As a way to fill in the space of your embarrassment, you tell her about how you received this. You tell her everything, and you don't expect her to understand; how could she. But she understands as well as she can, and—again—she is as real as you can imagine.

"How is his cock?" she says, peering down.

"Kite!" you yell.

"Surely you've thought of it, right?"

You lean back on your dresser, flushed, and Kite laughs.

Kite lives in Roseville in an apartment near Rosedale Mall. She lives by herself, works from home as a software engineer for a bank and enjoys painting ceramics and fucking shit up with her sword. She has two cats, Beelzebub and Asmodeus. She has a shrine to the red goddess Babalon in her living room. Some of the others she's met online in her women-only occult study group were reluctant to admit her. You can tell this hurt her, but also that she had no qualms in cursing them until they relented. She practices with her German longsword in the courtyard of her apartment, amidst the hanging laundry. One time when you're hanging out with her there, as she goes through her reps of parries, and you're drinking a beer and watching, she tells you that she admires you.

"Really?" you say. This takes you aback.

"Yeah," she says, placing her sword on the arms of a plastic chair. She runs her hands through her thick black hair in a ponytail—hair that you have to admit you're jealous about, compared to your own thinning blond-gray hair, even though you don't want to be jealous—and smiles, but shyly. "I've looked up to you. Like—you're farther along than I am with the transition. But not just that. That sounds like it's a matter of *time*. No, I just—" She holds out your hands. "You've just had to go through a lot more shit than I have. It's been more of a struggle for you, I know. But I still feel like shit, all the time! All the time."

"But, Kite," you say, "You're doing so well. You mean, you're a fucking rock star."

"Hah. Thanks." She picks up her sword again. "But it's a little more complicated than that. You turn every compliment—even from you—into something fake. Like they don't really mean anything. You mean, I get how some trans women just want to be left alone, you know? Like they disappear into the ether. You know how it looks like they're pulling the ladder up from underneath them. But I get it. You can't do that, but I get it."

A gaggle of twenty-year-old guys with hockey hair comes into the courtyard from the parking lot. They stop talking as soon as they see the two of you.

"That looks dangerous," one of them says to Kite, trying to chuckle or flirt.

"Damn right it is," she says. He thinks about saying something but snorts instead and heads into the building with his posse. These ordinary moments make you glad you're with a woman holding a longsword who knows how to use it. You figure it cuts down their stares and increases their own terror, anywhere from a third to a half. When you were masquerading as a man but hadn't realized you were a woman, you would be accounted for in those gaggles of men, but your confusion and panic was like a low-baud signal about being found out. (But why? You had no idea at the time.). It cast you as the "quiet one." You went along but you didn't have anywhere else to go.

On the other hand, when you'd find yourself in a group of women, you tried to become as invisible as possible. Nothing thrilled you more than when they forgot you were there, as they talked about men and the things they could talk about without men around. When they noticed you were there, it was like an invisibility switch turning off. Invisibility was a balm. But they would say, "Oh my god, deadname, I didn't realize you were here!"

"Haha, your secrets are safe with me!" you'd say, smiling and crestfallen.

"Do you want to hold it?" she said, offering me the sword.

"*Do I?*" you say with great exaggeration and flourish. "But please help me so I don't, you know . . ." You trail off.

"Cut off your arm?" Kite suggests.

"Yeah," you say. "That."

You hold the blade, wrapping your hands around the hilt. Kite shows you how. You feel, as you slowly raise it over your head, that in this moment in the courtyard you would be able to cut to the quick of anything.

*

Thinking of your past leaves you caught between two biozones—the industrialist voivodeship of woodland and rust where you grew up, and the heavily curated hyper-enclaves of the "creative class" which you currently circumlocute, if not fully occupy. As a trans woman, your distance from both has been acute. You have trouble imagining the former accepting you at all, and though the latter accepts anyone, theoretically, it is wholly dependent on money that you don't have, though you've been able to fake it in short bursts, especially when your writing career was getting off the ground, right before it was not getting off the ground and in fact cratering, killing-all-the-dinosaurs cratering.

Old Facebook friends ask for recommendations for nannies or au pairs on Facebook.

You forget that you are lucky too, privileged at birth. You try to remind yourself of this; you are not without a home or food or unbruised skin. And though the terror of assault is almost ever-present, it usually metastasizes into ridicule or contempt—snickers or deep evil glares.

Comparatively, you imagine that your old hometown would be immeasurably more difficult as a place to be a trans woman, simply for practical and demographic reasons. Maybe you're imagining wrong. You're glad you escaped it many years ago, though not without a little guilt for the trans people who *do* likely exist in your old hometown. You couldn't conceive of coming out as trans there, especially in those first few awkward, exhilarating months where every day felt like cliff-diving and you had no idea what you were doing with makeup. How would you survive? How would they survive? But they *do* survive—they work as piecework welders and grocery store clerks and salvagers into the outsourced earthquake fissures of the dying city like everyone else. It's like finding veterans of a distant long-forgotten war living in the house you grew up in. Sleeping in your childhood bed with the baseball pennants and the nightlight and the Huey Lewis and the News poster on the wall.

You wonder whether provincialism might not actually be an advantage in a few circumstances—in that, if one is the only trans person in a social circle, and likely the only trans person the social circle will ever meet, and as long as the social circle doesn't consist of radical evangelicals who consider trans people subhuman as part of a despairing eschatology, the trans person would be accepted as "unique." The cost, of course, would be that the "uniqueness" would be severely delimited by the confines of what a dying city could offer—a narrow band of offerings indeed. Not in terms of physical goods—in 20__, online shopping precludes the need for a vibrant retail "experience," urban or suburban, and if one needed "culture" transfusions there were a few mid-major American cities just a couple of hours away by car, which was nothing really (though when you drove to, say, Cleveland as a kid for a family excursion to the zoo, those cities felt emeraldine, even with the soot and the abandoned cars and storefronts constantly on the edge of your periphery). No, it would be more the dread about being around people who would accepted a trans person "as they were" but had an overpowering incuriosity to understand anything about being trans. The people you left behind have a mixture of bluster and inferiority complex that is a toxic combination when you're in any mode of self-discovery, let alone one as hairtrigger and pain-inducing as gender transition.

It's horrible to even think it, and this is why you could never go back there, except in uncomfortable familial circumstances, like your mother's protracted illness, or the funeral you imagine with dread.

Two days before your son's visit, you give him a call. Via Mary, of course, but she readily puts him on.

"Yeah, hello?" he says. You can tell he is pretending to not quite know who called him, or to be nonchalant about it.

"Hey, it's _____," you say.

"Oh, hey," he says. "How . . . how are you?"

"I'm fine, Aaron," you say. "And you?"

You can hear him shrugging on the phone.

"I'm okay. I hate Kansas," he says.

"Oh," you say. "How . . . how come?"

"I really hate it here," he says emphatically. "Everyone is mean. I mean, no one is really interested in hockey. But also . . ." He trails off. "I told a friend here that I have two moms, and he laughed at me. I got embarrassed and made him promise not to tell anyone else. And he would hold it over me. He'd smirk at me in the cafeteria."

You listen in horror, but you are glad he is telling you anything at all, and that he considers you his mother.

"What happened then?" you say, trying to keep your voice as level as possible.

"I didn't do anything. I held it in. But I feel worse. Now I just want to leave." He paused. "It hurts to hold it in."

"I know," you say, thinking back to the endless cabals of bullies at your schools. "Look, I really do."

And you tell him the story of the glass-bottom boat. You leave out a few of the more lurid details, of course, you don't say outright that they called you *faggot*, and he is quiet.

"That is . . . brutal," he says.

"Yeah," you say, and you ready yourself for some version of a pep talk. "But listen—those people don't get to define you. Only you do. They're weak. They're weaklings."

"I didn't even want to tell him that you used to be my dad," he says in a small voice.

"I know, kiddo. I know. It's okay." You start to tear up. You are allowed to tear up. For the next half hour you talk about the visit, and where he wants to go, and Minecraft, which he still does play after all. He didn't know why he lied about that, but you imagine that he wanted to seem older to you, and tougher, and a shooting game would let him appear that way. He broke down for you the qualities of about a half-dozen different mods.

That night after the poetry reading in your old home-town, you had a couple of drinks at a nearby dive bar (*all* bars downtown near the coffee shop were dive bars) with a friend who accompanied you to the read-ing, where thankfully you managed to bite your tongue and not harangue bitterly about your loss at the open mic. After saying goodbye you began your drive home. It was after two a.m. The night air kept sultry and there were, you remember, armadas of moths flittering every-where as you walked and, later, slapping against your car windshield at fifty miles an hour. You were on the outskirts of the city, still a mile from your parents', and had just gone underneath an arched concrete railroad bridge. That was when you saw a car in your rearview mirror accelerating rapidly toward you as if you were stationary inside the car waiting for a red light. The car didn't slow down and you prepared yourself, in the half-second this took to happen, to be rear-ended, and who knew what would have happened then.

The car didn't run into you but ran your tail inches from your bumper, and kept on you. You accelerated a little bit, and they kept on you. Everything was white-knuckle panic. You envisioned them in your head as joyriding, high kids, cackling like the bullies from your high school. This kind of brinksmanship was the type of bullying that happened all the time in school for you, though with fists instead of cars.

You thought that you were going to be run off the road, and who knew what would happen then. You saw up ahead the turnoff to your grandmother's trailer park and you made a sharp right into the gates of the Crystal Court. They followed. The lanes between the trailers were narrow, pivoted, and you turned left, then left again, then right—making your way to your grandmother's trailer, though she was sleeping peacefully and you had no idea whether you were going to wake her, and what she could do—call the police? While they beat you with pipes?

After the third turn, the car veered away at the same speed, and you made your way to your grandmother's little two-car parking area and cried and shivered. Though this could have happened anywhere, this incident was like the final seal on an apocalyptic scroll—signifying, along with the poetry reading, everything you hated about your hometown, presaging disaster were you to stay there. After that summer you never came back for more than a few days at a time.

For many years after your transition, after your mom started getting older, you were terrified of funerals, any funeral, in your old hometown. How they would see you—the old Polish and Italian families of your second cousins who stayed in town. How they would shun you. Or whether they would not know who you were in the first place. Maybe the penny would drop when they saw you in the front pew, a Polish church in a religion that despised you and considered you subhuman—or worse, as a confused man.

During your father's funeral, you were right on the cusp of coming out. You were so numb, and self-possessed with your own thoughts, that you had no space to process that your father was dead. He knew, though. He knew you were a woman. You told him a few months before he died. You had hoped for resolution with that, but he never spoke to you again.

Your mother would explain it away when you were on the phone or Skype; he was "busy" or "taking a nap" or "picking up a prescription" or "really not doing well." For her part, your mother accepted you grudgingly, in that she would talk to you, but she never quite understood, and only spoke of it in terms of your father and the harm and pain you were causing him. And then he died of a heart attack, and you gave in to your mother to "not rock the boat" by going to the funeral as deadname rather than _____. Your marriage was on the edge of the cliff as well, and Aaron hated you, and for three days in the town of your birth you pretended you were a perfectly normal, miserable little family. You shook hands with the cousins. Your anger at your parents was a wave that threatened to wash away everything you had tried to build for yourself, and with no place to put your anger, you withdrew. You wanted to be impregnable.

Instead when the wave rolled back, your old life was gone and your son was in Kansas.

How does love fulfill a desire? You have to figure this out on your own. But you wonder if love is not meant to—instead it is meant to make all desires sharper, more real.

The day before your son's visit, you receive a call from your hometown hospital. Your mother's illness has taken a sudden turn for the worse, the doctor says. She's been moved to hospice, and her time there should be brief, so it's best to come as soon as you can.

You are at your tiny kitchen table for two, and have no idea what feelings you should expect to have over the next few weeks, months, years.

You call your ex and explain what is happening, and could your son meet you in the town of your birth so he could say goodbye to his grandmother, who loved him very much. She agrees—she will come too. You say all right.

*

You hesitate, but you end up bringing the disassembled boyfriend with you, even though you'll have to pay for the extra baggage. He is like a talisman, like the three novels from the Weimar Republic that you keep in your carry-on, novels of wonder and slow panic. Just in case you want to dip into them. Break in case of emergency.

The feelings you possess are clear and sparse. Able to be crammed in a carry-on. On the rideshare to the airport, there's a parade of ATVs and pickup trucks going the other way, honking, men in the flatbeds with guns and flags. There's about a mile of them on the road, heading into the city—you can hear them shouting, honking their horns, blasting Toby Keith, Ares's men shouting. A few of the trucks make a U-turn on the interstate. You can practically hear the shouts. You lean forward in the car. Your driver's face is placid as you watch the three black trucks get closer and closer. They accelerate. They move into all three lanes. The highway has cleared of other cars. You can see the faces of the men—short cropped hair, sunglasses, black baseball caps. The flags whip and whip.

"Can you drive faster?" you say in a hissed whisper, but your driver doesn't look back at you and keeps the same steady pace. They come closer and closer. The doom approaches. You will never get off the ground. They will run you down, these men. You know them. They start honking. You can see their empty faces. You close your eyes and brace yourself. They turn off at the

exit that comes toward you suddenly, the exit leading into the city. You lean back in the seat and breathe
and—

*Interiority, possession, sovereignty, structure: all of
this can be yours*

When you reach your boarding gate, and watch the
throng crowding around the ticket counter on a Thurs-
day morning, everybody harried, you remember the last
time you were on a plane and the embarrassment that
came with it, an embarrassment that, as it rushes into
you, feels like a cold case reopened on account of new
evidence. You were on a commuter plane—a prop plane
from the regional airline you were taking to visit your
parents; this was before your father died—and you saw
that your seat was in the first row. You were elated for a
few minutes and told your wife, who was traveling with
you, that you both had been bumped up to first class
for the first time in your lives, and you were trying to
impart onto your wife your happiness. But this curdled
into sheepishness when you realized that the plane was
too small for first class. The two of you sat in silence as
the plane took off.

This tiny luxurious possibility had meant something to you, and it hurt that you had something taken
away that you never had to begin with. It was so stupid,
but as you watched the checkerboarded soybean fields
float underneath you, you held your wife's hand tight
and wondered—was she feeling the same as you? As

embarrassed? Was she anticipating a little extra liber-
tine's attention from a flight attendant on a fifty-minute
flight, and was found wanting and saddened? For being
so unlike a business class traveler or couple traveling
to an airport hub only to go to somewhere more exotic
than the Rust Belt city that groaned and died a tiny bit
more with each passing year?

You never did find out. And since then, you have
become a woman, and are no longer a husband; and
certainly not a wife.

The airport is shaped as if several long-barreled shot-
guns have been duct-taped together at the stock. It feels
dangerous as you weave between people on the mov-
able walkway to catch your flight. You feel only trace
amounts of peril from the other passengers on the walkway with you, but much more from the state troopers,
the border patrol agents with AR-15s slung over their
backs as they stand in line for Starbucks, on break,
but ready for anything. Everywhere is a border now.
You know more than one trans woman yanked from a
security checkpoint because the opportunity to humili-
ate them was too tempting. The agents go to churches,
where they hear warnings about you and others like you.
They know enough to be afraid.

When you enter the boarding gate you skirt around
the edges of the other travelers. The security line could
have been much worse for you. No existential pushback
from TSA. Your ID had been changed two years ago,
right before air travel became much more difficult for
trans people. And even you had to push and pull with

the courts. The TSA agents ten minutes before were so tired and bored and mournful when you took off your floral flats and put them in the gray bin. They were too tired to be proud about any "gotcha" moments about you. Then your purse. You wear a solid black dress, to the knees. You want to be read as feminine as possible, even though jeans—or, hell, leggings—would have been a lot more comfortable. No jewelry.

And at the boarding gate you scan the sixty or so people milling around waiting to board, and take a quick guess as to how they consider you:

Forty-five pay you no mind at all.

Ten glance at you, but then turn back to their phones, their boarding passes, their children; or if they are children, their parents.

Four keep staring at you. Two of these are trying not to make it seem like they're staring at you. The other two are unrepentant, but more from curiosity or even a dull shock—that you are sharing the same space as them—as opposed to malice.

And there is one man, the remaining man, who glares. He crosses his arms. You turn away, look at the clock, turn back toward him—as if trying to reset a screen that's frozen—and he still glares. Black T-shirt from an auto body shop from a red state, scuffed jeans, long beard peppered with gray. Bald. Thick copper rings on his fingers. In times like this you have no idea what to do or say. You find a place to sit down, on the other side of the throng, next to the lone phone recharging station of what seems like the entire concourse, where men and women in suits congregate, like savannah herd animals around a watering hole. You look up once from your phone, and he still stares at you even though his view is mostly obscured. These people are the ones that usually fill you with dread. In the cramped space of the boarding gate you feel your body begin to coil and electrify, which powers up something around you, though you're not entirely sure what. The airport smells like ozone, fried calamari appetizers, and cleaning spray. You turn your head slightly to focus on the control tower outside the plate glass window, its red lights shining like garnets, and the column of storm clouds beyond it, which you and the other sixty will be flying into.

Gold Status members, and any of our guests with special needs or small children, can now begin to board.

You call Kite. She's working in her second job, as a security guard this week at a strip mall bank in outer Stillwater.

"I can't do this," you say. "There's a guy in the boarding area that wants to murder me. He wants to murder me, Kite."

"Deep breaths," Kite says. "You got this."

"Yeah, but—"

"He does not matter," she said. "Your mom matters. Your son matters. He's not going to hurt you. The sick fucker might glare but there's nothing he can do."

"Yeah," I breathe.

"You breathed! I mean . . . I heard it. Good job."

Airplanes are gambling houses. There's a lack of control with them. When you are in the sky, you look to your right, in the aisle seat, at the glaring man, and you expect him to say something, but he doesn't. Of course his assigned seat is next to yours. *Of course.* He's not looking at you, though. It's as if you're not there, which is a relief. You expect the worst kinds of conversations and venom to emanate from his mouth. Instead he takes out black earbuds from his jacket pocket and plugs them into his phone, and leans the seat back.

The airplane flies into the cloudbank, engulfed in the godwall. The airplane's rivets rattle as it climbs. You close your eyes too and can't relax. Your mother is going to die soon. You imagine a map of the United States with dots and dashes from far-flung states converging on the town of your birth, along with all the other, more frequent travelers crisscrossing the globe, or returning from such an act.

This is also the first time you've been in your hometown as yourself.

A lot has changed there—for example, you've read they have been so desperate for jobs there that California has outsourced its earthquake activity to the city.

Folks, we're going to be experiencing a little turbulence—

You hear a noise from beside you. The man isn't sleeping. He's whimpering. Another noise: there's a child crying a couple of rows behind you, then the noise of a father trying to hush a son desperately. But you think that he is less trying to soothe his child than to soothe himself.

"We're going to die," the man beside you says between clenched teeth. "We're going to fucking die die *die.*"

Yes, you think. *Probably not today, though.*

The airplane keeps climbing. The man's face exudes sweat. His hands open and close like pincers.

Folks, thanks for flying with us today. You won't be able to see it, on account of the clouds, but we're juuuust passing over New York City on route to our destination.

You look down despite yourself, and see nothing but clouds. You're not entirely sure why New York City is below you, as it's nowhere near the flight path, a path over long since decimated peoples that mostly only remain in the names of states, rivers, and malls.

There is a teenage soldier in the seat ahead of you, in crisp Army camouflage, who presses his face against the window, whispering something to himself, perhaps in awe or anger at the megapolis he can't see, which shouldn't be there. You don't know if he's coming or going from his war. The man beside you presses the flight attendant's button, moving his arm very slowly, trying to keep steady.

He wants to purchase alcohol.

"Sir," the summoned flight attendant says, "you'll be on the ground in about . . ." She checks her watch. "Forty minutes?" She's a woman about your age, hair in a bun, red dress. She looks desperately tired. Her eyes flicker to you for a second, before fixating on the man, who seems like he wants to shake her untroubled calm all the way down to the ground.

He shakes his head desperately, as if a commanding officer is denying him battlefield medicine. He pulls a ten-dollar bill out of his pocket and hands it to the flight attendant. You vaguely remember other times when people have ordered alcohol on short flights, and you've always taken it as a splurge of indolence, but this man seems to be in panic mode.

"You are tasked with offering a variety of in-flight beverages, either for free or for a small surcharge," he says, in a clenched-jaw monotone. "At this time I would like to partake in such an offering. I am planning on giving you cash—for you only take cash and don't give change back—to complete this transaction."

You are beginning to have pity on the glarer (why, though, he probably still hates the very thought of you), and apparently the flight attendant does too, because she sighs and takes the ten-dollar bill and in a minute returns with a plastic cup of orange juice and a miniature bottle of vodka. The size of those bottles always fills you with glee, as if there are clandestine distilleries operated by mice. The man nods grimly, and downs the vodka, and then the orange juice. He opens his tray, smooths it with his hands, and places the empty bottle and cup on it, leaning back and closing his eyes.

The intercom crackles.

Folks, we'rrrre almost out of this turbulence. Below you, if you squint in juuuuust the right way, you'll be able to see San Francisco beneath you. The Golden Gate City, to your right, and to your left as well. Tantalizingly close, isn't it? Looks like we'll be out of this headwind and be able to reach the ground a little early, and have you on your way, whether _____ is your final destination or if you're catching a connecting flight. Check with your gate agent after you land.

A pause. No one except the soldier in front of you tries to peer out the window to view San Francisco, or try. The baby has hushed even.

Also, folks, the control tower has let us know that if you're trying to make a connection to the past, please see your gate agent.
You may need to make other arrangements.
"Fuck," the soldier mutters to himself.

Perhaps your past is what you're flying toward, the past when you were an embryonic male, when thinking of yourself as *transgender* would have been completely unfathomable. The few times as a teenager when you had tried on your mother's lingerie, drunk on peach schnapps, were unmoored from identity, any sense of *this is who you are* since you had no idea who you were, and were in no position to even pretend you were something you weren't. Moments like floating islands, like ghost ships. The plane shudders. Plenty of other moments that you kept pushing down. But they come back to you, in shorn pieces, 25,000 feet above Lake Michigan. You start remembering the endless hours of disassociating that began when you were six or seven, when you would soothe yourself to sleep by creating elaborate dreamworlds, whose stories would chain together for weeks, months. You kept doing this until you were in college. The knowledge that you were pretending to be a man wouldn't come till much later.

"Hold my hand," the man sitting next to you says, breaking you away from your thoughts. He doesn't look at you.
"I'm sorry?" you say, startling, though you know exactly what he said.

"Hold my hand, ma'am," he says. "Please. I'm scared."
"Why were you staring at me?" you say. "At the
boarding gate? *I* was scared."
He says nothing. You don't take his hand. You notice
his smell for the first time, in this cramped intimacy,
sandalwood dollar-store deodorant, and he says:
"I started listening to my music, but it's not my
music. It's a stream of a voice. I think it's your guard-
ian angel. I don't believe in angels, or God. Any of it. But
from this, I think God is the servant of the angels, and
not the other way around."
"What does the voice say?" you whisper.
The clouds break. The plane begins descending.
Unfurling below you is your old hometown, huddled
against the Great Lake filled with storms and ship-
wrecks, all the roofs gray, the empty brown blocks where
all the houses had been razed, the cars edging around
the sinkholes in the streets. Only the cinderblock tav-
erns are still open and viable.
"The voice said that its name is ORIOLE. It told
me everything about me. What I was doing before my
return trip back to _____, the name of the camp-
site I stayed at, the name of the girl I fucked, what she
smelled like, how many drugs we both took, the drugs'
street and scientific names, the colors in my eyes when
we stared at the moonlight on our backs among the
trash and pine trees and smoke and how the girl's boyfriend found us, and didn't attack me but her, because I
know how men like that are, they take the path of least
resistance and he had a fucking bullwhip, and she was
screaming in the dark and I just ran, I didn't even try
to help her, I ran into the woods, and the woods were

full of violet sparks which I'm pretty sure were from the drugs, but the sparks were coming from the pine trees and the owls' eyes. I heard shouting behind me and Slipknot somewhere in the woods, I started running toward it, I hoped those were my people playing the Slipknot, I left that girl behind, I left her behind. I keep following the Slipknot, I stumbled down a ravine—"

Though you did not touch his hand, there's a chill there. You rub your hand to shake the warmth back into it.

"When I know who I am again, when I *come to*, I'm in the airport. This is what the voice told me, about what happened, and all of it's true. It's all true. And the voice also told me that it's possible that *I'm not even really here*, in this airplane flying, that I might exist as a reflection of your own painful memory of bullies. That my body isn't flesh and blood as much as it is a wiki."

"You mean, like, Wikipedia?" you say, trying to follow. He squeezes his hand; he was probably trying to squeeze yours but didn't realize it wasn't there.

"I don't know! The voice said that we all were wikis, collections of facts and recounted events and time-stamps, that everything I did in the forest was in the wiki, and that we were dark blue wikis that were bundled together into an even larger wiki, and that the other animals were dark red wikis and the plants were dark green wikis and so on. And that any of them can be edited, by anyone, but you have to have the right username and password, even to edit your own wiki, but that you . . ." He turns toward you for the first time. "*You* were able to change yours, in fact you changed *a lot*, even though it might not seem like it for you, not just being a girl now, but that your change history was like an aria, and that . . ." He took a deep breath.

"And then the angel told me to leave you the fuck alone. I started to panic. I am panicking. I'm in your wiki too now, me telling this to you. It's part of your story now, and I'm sorry. I'm a total fuck-up and that girl is probably in the hospital or dead because of me. But this is what the voice said to me, and now I just want to get off this fucking plane and I'm sorry."

You didn't think you deserved any care from Oriole.

You stare at him, and the first impulse is to say, *That's all right,* or *I understand!* or even *I'm sorry you're going through this, it must be horrible.* In the past you have been good at glossing things over. But as the plane's landing gear drops, you unbuckle your seat belt. The flight attendant, who's walking the aisle making sure everyone's safely buckled in, shakes her head at you and frowns.

You say to her: "I'd like to change my seat, please." And she knows. She knows why, and she grabs your hand and both of you float toward the back of the plane, and you don't really have the time to wonder why Oriole is still looking out for you, since you thought you had failed them, and your trans sisters, in some fundamental way. But you will take it. You will take any help you can get. Some things can't be solved; all you can do is leave. Rather than jumping out of the plane, which wouldn't work out well for you, your guide escorts you to the only empty seat in the plane, near the back, and you strap yourself in.

"Thank you," you whisper.

The flight attendant nods and smooths out the creases of her red uniform.

The seat belt is tight against your breasts, smallish as they are, and though it's uncomfortable, it reminds you how much your body has changed since the last time you've come home.

And here, you will see your son as well. And how he will see you will undoubtedly be different.

As you take a deep breath and look down through the window, you see your old hometown as a tableau: the tiny gray houses and block after abandoned block, given up to weeds and stunted trees, burnt-down houses and blackened lots like funeral offerings, and at last visible there's the earthquake fissure running the length of 12 Street, a miles-long abyss that has split the city in half, bottomless as far as you can see. The city you once loved and hated when you were a man has this scar, you share scars then, your scars are named and filed away and perhaps this abyss below you is named in the wiki of the earth, though whether this one will heal, like yours have begun to, is anyone's guess.

How can you imagine yourself here.

Taking the rental Nissan Sentra from the airport, all of your past here unspools. Every thread. Your boy past, and all the past you weren't a part of. The sky is gray, unyielding. The great blizzards, the woods behind your house that was stolen by the French Empire, their crumbled forts that had dissolved into archaeological imprints, if that. The four boys in your Boy Scout troop who died in a very short span of time: car accident in snow, drunk driver while walking on road, killed while on ATV, hunting accident. The woodsmoke, the trash burning on the edge of the woods. The mountain of a landfill that was the highest point in the county and the baseball diamond tucked into the incline proudly sponsored by Waste Management.

You were never sure if they found the tallest hill in the county and carved it like dividing a geode and then put in the garbage or if they built the landfill from scratch and put some dirt-padding on its visible face to make it seem less awful. You took that road every day on the bus into high school, where the boys would torture you, but now you are driving on 12th Street, abandoned lots adjoined with the abandoned factories, running parallel to the deep crevice that, aside from the plaza of casinos along I-90, generates income for the city. On the east side of the city it is perhaps even worse—many bridges and roadways are not serviced anymore. The roadways and bridges have become uneasy places to place tents and RVs from the 1990s. Almost every year has a long winter, though they have been getting warmer, more erratic. The wrecks of the sailing ships underneath the waves that chop like machetes. The fishing industry that died in the early twentieth century. The steel industry that died in the late. The breweries that died. The plastics and light manufacturing industry that died. The service industry that died. And there are no funerals for these deaths, only broken tombstones, and your own memories of the wreckage. When you were a child the paper mill would make the whole east side of town smell like sulfur from the wood chip pulping. You got used to it. Everyone got used to it. The mill cleaved off three of your uncle's fingers with an industrial paper cutter, and you were used to that too. Soon enough the paper mill closed, was itself liquidated.

It starts to rain. The rain is cold. Unspool, unspool. You grew here. You grew in the shadow of your parents, a deep shadow and a touch disastrous. They loved you. You were so angry at them, all the time. You couldn't articulate that they weren't well. Anxieties would come to the fore unbidden for all of you at once, like the aria the man on the plane said. The aria would shine when you were at McDonald's with your parents, and you were embarrassed to be there with them, because you were back from an expensive college on a scholarship, and your mom started to cry. She saw your embarrassment right away. Your dad stared at you, as if he couldn't believe that you would do something so horrible to your mother. You sighed and looked for a way out. There was none. Not then. You pushed your own shame down. After many decades it had compressed into a black diamond. When at last you were able to extract it, and hold it in your hands, after you started your transition, you applied pressure to it with your fingers and it cracked like an egg.

Alchemy is much scarier than "alchemists" say.

"Well," your mom says, "it looks like you're here."

"I *am*," you say, sitting down next to her bed and crossing your legs. Smiling. Face flushed. Your boyfriend is still in your carry-on. He is heavy. You had thought about putting him together in the airport bathroom, but you didn't know how you could pull that off. And your reserves of energy were too low.

And then you decided, *fuck it,* he wasn't coming out.

"You're probably not going to stay for long," she says, coughing.

You want to say: *long enough* but nothing comes out. You don't want to be the ungrateful daughter that used to be a son.

"As long as it takes," you say.

"What is that supposed to mean?" she says, squinting. "Are you checking your watch waiting for me to keel over?"

"No, Mom, that's not what I meant . . ."

"Ah, well, it's probably my time soon anyway." She wipes her nose on her sleeve. "You can have my jewelry. If you want it. You don't know, maybe it's not your style."

You know this whiplash of anger and self-pity all too well.

You let out a deep breath from a secret temple inside your diaphragm that you saw in a YouTube video once. "I love you, Mom."

She turns toward the ceiling-high window of the hospice. They built the hospice right next to one of the crevices. Lookout Springs, they called it. Ever since your old hometown started taking on more affluent cities' natural disasters, the grid has been a hodgepodge of storms and seismic activity.

"And where is my grandson?" she says, still not looking at you. "Are you holding him out on me?"

"No—he's . . . he's coming, Mom. With Mary. They were having trouble with the weather so they're stuck in Chicago."

You were reluctant to have Mary come this way, all this way, but you saw no other way to get your son here. This wasn't the seventies, when a child could be given a note around his neck and sent alone on a long journey, as in a fairy tale.

You try to see your mother's face in yours now. The similarities were always there, even when you were living as a man. A boy. You "took after her." Though you always had the temper of your dad, you took on your mother's worries but also, you realized, her tenderness. You allow yourself to think that.

OKPsyche

"I never understood why you left her," she said, closing her eyes and almost cooing. It's probably true that she's saying this to you. But there's a slim chance that she's *not*, so you stay quiet.

The window rattles. The air in the facility smells like condensed milk. You lean forward and put your hand on it, trying to quell the glass. There's a tower on each end of the crevice, and a spindly black bridge stretching over the yaw. Red and white lights flash on top of the towers, and the bridge shakes. A boxy thing that looks like a cable car rises up toward the center of the bridge. You haven't seen the cables against the dark background before.

"Oh, that racket," your mother says, opening her eyes and rubbing her forehead. "What possessed them to build a hospice here is beyond me." She looks at a portrait of your dad on the dresser, as if seeking counsel from him.

The cheapest land? you think. Everything is so fragile. Passing on/passing through. Your mom is not mean-spirited but she's in a ton of pain, at least until the hospice gave her neo-morphine, which makes her visible emotions dully flow.

"Can I get you some water, mom?"

"Yes, that would be lovely, deadname. Thank you, dear."

Hands shaking, you get a little water into one of the tiny Dixie cups stacked near the sink.

"No, not that shit. Jesus, son—sorry—no one's been able to drink the tap water here in a decade. There's a little bottled water in the mini-fridge. I'm sorry. I shouldn't call you son. I should know better. But I guess I have too many things on my mind right now."

135

The cable car trundles toward your end of the crevice and pivots, tipping out salvage.

You wonder: does *she* see herself in *you*?

You love your family. Your mother is dying. It's inevitable and yet unimaginable.

"I miss your father," your mother says, looking out the window. "He would hate this. He would fuss over me."

"I know," I say. "I miss him too." Sometimes the platitudes make up for missed opportunities. You think about telling her about your encounters with him, and the camera obscura, but you hold on to those thoughts.

"And he loved you," she says. "He really did. Thick and thin. He really did. Even when he never showed it."

"I . . . know that too," you manage to say.

"You know he had a rough childhood," she says. "His parents—your grandparents—were both alcoholics."

"I know," you say.

"And he lived in the house with the two of them while his siblings had moved out and fought in the war."

"Mom, I *know*." Your father told you how unhappy he was when you were a child. You remember the adage: *Believe a man when he tells you who he is for the first time.*

You pause. "It wasn't easy for you either."

She turns her head from you. "No," she said. She grabs your hand. "But you deserved better. I mean, later—when you changed."

You look at her and squeeze her hand as gently as you can. A nurse comes in with tulips. Mary calls. Everything blurs together, and also away.

*

Ten years before, before they built the chasm, you had gone with your parents down to one of the beaches where a creek ran into Lake Erie, and you'd look for beach glass together. Your mom told you that, back when she was a girl, she would go to this beach, and there would be plenty of beautiful shards of milky viridian and egg-shell blue. But over the decades it became picked over, and people stopped using glass. Still, people seemed to have forgotten it again when the three of you went. You remember your mother's momentary, impossible serenity cutting you, watching her from a small distance away, as she rolled up her trousers and flitted through the coarse sand with her hands, looking for the glass the waves slowly beat into smoothed shapes. Sharp edges that could lacerate skin worn down into curves. In your apartment you have a mason jar half-filled with the beach glass from this single trip: a marvelous trea-sure. One time when your son was staying at your tiny one-bedroom apartment right after the divorce, before Mary moved to the other state, you watched him knock over your beach glass and send it tumbling throughout your living room/foyer/kid's bedroom. And you yelled at him, full-throated. You are not blameless. No. You would never claim that. For months you would find little pieces of driftglass when you cleaned, and you are sure you lost several. Aaron said nothing to you. He was seven. And then he was gone.

You watched your father along the gentle banks of the creek, hands on his hips, watching the two of you. He would occasionally scoop out sand looking for the beach glass but since he was too high up on the shore, he found nothing and grimaced. You waved at him. He waved back. You were still acting and appearing as a man, though the foundations of your life that you carefully hoped to keep intact forever started to develop hairline cracks, on account of the tremoring deep inside your body as you slept.

Does Psyche find her way back home, from the honeysuckle borderlands? Does she have a husband, the one who fumbled for her in the dark? Is she the bride of desire itself? Does Venus leave her the fuck alone? Is she immortal from ambrosia? Is she scarred? Is the image of her escape and future prosperity going to last? She remembers how she had to bring back Persephone's beauty for Aphrodite, as a final task: when she opened the box that contained her beauty, there was only death inside. And so Psyche died. Cupid saved her, and revived her, and Psyche became the goddess of the soul. But how did the beauty turn into death in the first place? And in this alleged ending, when she turns over in bed and sees Cupid there, arm draped over her, she thinks what would have happened if there was not a man to save her, and how she might have saved herself.

It's midnight. You keep checking your phone for flight updates but the chasm has scrambled your network, and you can't get a signal. You hear your mother's ragged breathing. You hold her hand.

"Mom, I love you," you whisper.

She murmurs, from a place deep inside her chest.

You think about getting a hotel room, but instead you keep vigil. You don't want to fall asleep on the unyielding couch but you do, right before dawn. You have a dream that you are lying in your bed in the house where you grew up, the Cape Cod with the red vinyl siding in the middle of nowhere. You're in your upstairs bedroom with the slanted attic roof. But you are yourself. Your legs hang over the side of the kid-sized bed. There's a girl at the foot of the bed. She's translucent yet fully there at the same time. She has blond, curly hair and smiles at you. You had this dream as a child, you remember—in fact, it never seemed like a dream to you at all, but rather a half-awake slumber that was as real as you were ever going to be. Is this the lost girl? Is this the psyche of the lost girl, the breath of the girl who you wanted to be? It has to be. It has to be. You don't want to be completely asleep, but rather half-awake and surfacing, the hypnopompic state where you slowly break from water into air—

your Rhine, your Lake of the Isles, your Styx, your Volga, your Great Lake—

and your thoughts about who you are comply with the breath of the girl you are. You struggle to wake. When you do wake up, your mother is dead.

After the hospice makes the arrangements, and you thank everyone, and cry for an hour, you change into black leggings and a Georgia Satellites T-shirt and head toward the chasm with your luggage. It's about nine o'clock in the morning. There is a fence around the perimeter but no one is working, because it's Sunday, the Lord's Day, so it's easy to find a break in the fence and slide through. It's a little harder with your luggage but you manage. You bump along right to the edge of the chasm.

You kneel and open your suitcase. You expect to see your father again, standing beside you, but it's just you. Maybe it's always been just you. Your boyfriend— still disassembled—lies in wait. One by one you toss the pieces of his slightly warm body over the edge.

How will it happen, in the end? For you to be possessed by your own heart?

"It's not your fault," you whisper, right before you toss over the head and torso. You think about what Oriole and your other benefactors would think about this—but maybe this was the point of sending the unassembled boyfriend to you after all. You hear him tumble, hitting the sides of the near endless ravine. You imagine Kite giving you a thumbs up from afar. You wonder what the excavators down there will think of the body parts drifting down into the abyss, before they turn back to their toil.

You book a hotel there at the edge of the chasm. You make your way to the foot of State Street, to pick up a cab to take you back to the hotel. No one knows your mother has died. Your son stands at the front desk. You take him up in your arms and after a second's stiffness, he relents. He is so much older than you remember. God, he is older.

After you let go, you stare at him for a few seconds.

"Where's your mom?" you say, without thinking.

In front of me, you desperately want him to say, to gently correct you. *Oh, you mean my* other *mom.*

"She's calling someone." He pauses. "Is grandma dead?"

You nod. "I'm sorry, Aaron. I'm so sorry. Let's . . . well, there's a Starbucks across the street. Do you want a cake pop or . . ." You struggle to remember what they have on the menu. "Well, whatever you want." You pause. You're fumbling, falling into the lionprayer air. You keep going. You arrest your fall for a second. "You feel okay?"

He rushes toward you and embraces you again.

"I don't feel okay," he says into your sleeve.

"I don't either," you say, the tears coming. "But it's okay."

You love him, you love him, you love him.

Acknowledgments

I've been working on this book for many years—at first it wasn't even a book, much less a short novel—and there are many people to thank:

My family, including my parents and siblings, and especially Ally and Toby, who have taught me so much as a mom and a human being.

Corie, my anchor and my love. Couldn't do this without you at my side.

Heather Shaw and Megha Majumdar for publishing excerpts as short stories in *Persistent Visions* and *Catapult*, respectively, and providing such a good home for them.

Isaac Fellman, for encouragement at a crucial point in the life of the book; Suzan, for ceaseless friendship and solidarity; and all the folks at the Minnesota Transgender Health Coalition support group.

And the Minnetonka Ladies, Jessie Hennen and Christine Utz, without whom I would be lost, utterly lost, in finding a shape and a full voice in this book with countless rounds of revisions.

About the Author

Anya Johanna DeNiro is a trans woman and a speculative fiction writer living in Saint Paul, Minnesota. She is the author of *City of a Thousand Feelings,* which was on the Honor Roll for the Otherwise Award.

Reconstruction: Stories
Alaya Dawn Johnson
HURSTON/WRIGHT LEGACY AWARD FINALIST

"Haunting, not just for its vividness, but also
for how Johnson writes around felt
and imagined absences."
— *Chicago Review of Books*

Alien Virus Love Disaster: Stories
Abbey Mei Otis
NEUKOM DEBUT LITERARY AWARD SHORTLIST
PHILIP K. DICK AWARD FINALIST
BOOKLIST TOP 10 DEBUT SF&F

"An exciting voice. . . . dreamy but with an
intense physicality." — *Washington Post*
Best Science Fiction & Fantasy of the year

Ambiguity Machines: Stories
Vandana Singh
PHILIP K. DICK AWARD FINALIST
LOCUS RECOMMENDED READING LIST

"Singh breathes new life into the themes of
loneliness, kinship, love, curiosity, and the
thirst for knowledge. *Ambiguity Machines and
Other Stories* is a literary gift for us all."
— Rachel Cordasco, *World Literature Today*

In Other Lands: a novel
Sarah Rees Brennan
ALA RAINBOW BOOK LIST, JUNIOR LIBRARY
GUILD SELECTION, GEORGIA PEACH & FLORIDA
TEENS READ AWARD NOMINEE, MYTHOPOEIC,
HUGO, & LOCUS AWARD FINALIST

"Best of all, over four years in the otherlands,
Elliot grows from a defensive, furious,
grieving child into a diplomatic, kind,
menschy hero."
— *New York Times Book Review*

Spirits Abroad: Stories
Zen Cho
LA TIMES RAY BRADBURY PRIZE WINNER

"Absolutely gorgeous. . . . Just as with her novels, Cho merges humor and relatable characters with delightful prose and engaging storylines."
—Margaret Kingsbury, *Buzzfeed*

Never Have I Ever: Stories
Isabel Yap
BRITISH FANTASY AWARD WINNER
LADIES OF HORROR FICTION AWARD WINNER

"Monstrous, scary, joyful, unexpected, inventive, eerie and weird."
— Karla Strand, *Ms. Magazine*

Dance on Saturday: Stories
Elwin Cotman
PHILIP K. DICK AWARD FINALIST
NPR BEST OF THE YEAR

"My two favorite stories make up about half the book: 'Seven Watsons' and the title story both deliver all the sophistication and complexity of a novel at a third of the length, and center Black joy and endurance."— Amal El-Mohtar, NPR

Tender: Stories
Sofia Samatar
NPR BEST OF THE YEAR

"This is a short story collection containing wonder after wonder, done with casual intensity. These are all sharp knives of stories."
— Maria Dahvana Headley, *Electric Lit*

ALSO AVAILABLE FROM SMALL BEER PRESS

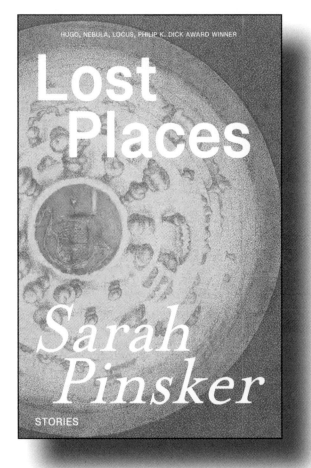

Lost Places: Stories
Sarah Pinsker

★ "Queer, hopeful, and eerie." — *Booklist* (starred review)

"Many of these stories involve people who've misplaced themselves:
in the wilderness, in the fog of dementia, in
strange circumstances. Pinsker's characters always make the
best of tricky situations, which only makes their struggles in
her topsy-turvy worlds more heartbreaking."
— Charlie Jane Anders, *Washington Post*